ADVANCE PRAISE FOR

A Thousand and One Nights

"Wonderful and incisive, *A Thousand and One Nights* tells us in a new way what it means to be young and American. Tupper casts a keen, intelligent eye on the contemporary world, its multitude of fakeries and deceits, providing us with a witty, poignant, wholly worthwhile read."

—Elizabeth Strout, author of *Abide with Me*
and *Amy and Isabelle*

"*A Thousand and One Nights* presents us with a compelling tour of the ersatz, dismally funny, and faintly depressing world of the third-tier entertainer: a tour that's beautifully understated in its emotional intelligence, and wry and clear-eyed and psychologically astute in its portrait of a young couple for whom getting through the day means not facing what's missing, whether from their act or their relationship. This is a moving and accomplished first novel."

—Jim Shepard, author of *Project X*

"An intriguing, often funny, and richly atmospheric novel...It is sharply observed, fresh and authentic in its vision, poignant in its depiction of a couple's willed facade and great fun to read...A one-of-a-kind book, fascinating and honest."

—Joan Silber, author of *Ideas of Heaven*
(National Book Award Finalist)

"*A Thousand and One Nights* lays bare the hopes and hearts of twenty-somethings yearning for success, adventure and love, and coming up just a little shy on all three counts... A moving account of finding yourself amid the detritus of your dreams."   —C. J. Hribal, author of *The Company Car*

"The problem of living even half-honestly in a world of routine cheating and of faked performance is a real one, and gives *A Thousand and One Nights* its vital center. Lara Tupper is a writer of many gifts, with a terrific story to tell."
                    —Judith Grossman, author of *Her Own Terms*

"Lara Tupper's first novel is music to the ear. It's travel, too, full of dark corners and poignant wit, a rich international coming of age, boozy nights and friendship, love. And Tupper is a kind of women's Rick Moody, her heroine more or less enslaved on a cruise ship, singing in too-heavy dresses, always making her way home." —Bill Roorbach, author of *Big Bend*

"A surprising look into an unfamiliar world."
                    —Alison Lurie, author of the Pulitzer
                    Prize–winning *Foreign Affairs*

"A clever tale of a young woman's witty, dissolute, and sometimes desperate tryst with overseas stage-act fame, *A Thousand and One Nights* shines with the poignant honesty of a pop song singer who can't quite get her life in key... A delightful first novel."
        —Kim Ponders, author of *The Art of Uncontrolled Flight*

A Thousand and One Nights

LARA TUPPER

A Thousand and One Nights

A HARVEST ORIGINAL
HARCOURT, INC.
Orlando   Austin   New York   San Diego   Toronto   London

www.HarcourtBooks.com

"Introduction" by A. S. Byatt, copyright © 2001 by A. S. Byatt, from *The Arabian Nights,* translated by Sir Richard F. Burton. Used by permission of Modern Library, a division of Random House, Inc.

Library of Congress Cataloging-in-Publication Data

Tupper, Lara.
A thousand and one nights/Lara Tupper.—1st ed.
p.   cm.
"A Harvest original."
1. Singers—Fiction.   2. Cruise ships—Fiction.   3. China—Fiction.
4. Middle East—Fiction.   I. Title.
PS3620.U74T46   2007
813'.6—dc22   2006008700
ISBN-13: 978-0-15-603092-2   ISBN-10: 0-15-603092-6

Text set in Minion
Designed by Linda Lockowitz

Printed in the United States of America

First edition
K J I H G F E D C B A

For my parents, who let me see places.

Scheherazade saves her own life by telling the king…
a thousand and one interwoven stories, which are
always unfinished at dawn—so deferring the execution
daily.…Human beings tell stories—in bars, in novels,
in courtship.…Scheherazade keeps her own life going.

—A. S. Byatt, Introduction to *The Arabian Nights:*
Tales from a Thousand and One Nights

A Thousand and One Nights

ONE

Rodgers and Hammerstein

IT STARTED ON A CRUISE SHIP, where nothing was exactly real. The brass railings of the lobby staircase were molded industrial plastic, liberally coated with copper-colored paint. The ship's largest funnel, visible from up to ten nautical miles, bore the company insignia in gleaming white and blue; it led nowhere, funneled nothing. The pool, deemed "refreshing" in the travel agent brochure, was waist-deep, heavily chlorinated, and too cold even for children. In a pinch, plastic ice sculptures were used for the Midnight Buffet. Stored in freezers and splashed with ice water to simulate melting drips, the statuettes (dolphin, starfish, palm tree) were appropriately cold to the touch. The slot machines were fixed to a timer; the bingo numbers were decided well in advance of the daily call. The rum punch was 80 percent Kool-Aid. And the surly pop duo in the Tally-Ho Lounge played to synthesized backing tracks.

AT THE TIME OF her Boston audition for Dancers Who Sing and Singers Who Move Well, Karla, who considered herself the latter, was three months out of music school and still living with her college roommate in Somerville, Massachusetts. The summer run of temping and tryouts had been humbling, until the cruise ship auditions began. The cruise reps seemed to care less about Karla's dance experience and more about her "people skills." They asked if she'd ever worked in the service industry, and Karla certainly had. Her three summers as Head Waitress at Cabbage Island Clambakes were suddenly three summers well spent.

Karla got a callback, her first ever, and then another. She had to give a quiz to imaginary poolside guests, using a microphone. She had to lead her fellow auditionees in an impromptu aerobics class. She had to fend off an angry passenger, played by the choreographer, who demanded a pillow made of goose down rather than foam.

She got it. She would be an Entertainer, according to her contract. She was hired to sing and dance and travel—she was going to be *paid* for this. She was twenty-two years old.

As it turned out, and as she might have guessed from the audition, Karla was required to sing and dance at night and to host Ping-Pong and Shuffleboard tournaments during the day. She didn't actually know how to keep score for Ping-Pong, but the passengers were drunk, merry, forgiving. Their first cruise! Karla usually nominated a teenage boy to keep track, and then gave him a rum punch as reward. It was that kind of ship: bang for the buck, affordable for families, nothing too exotic in the way of itineraries—Mediterranean in the summer, Caribbean in the winter. It was a British cruise line, and she was the only American to accept the contract. The main show, *Hound Doggin'*, a thinly veiled *Grease*, required at least one genuine American accent. The show-stopper was an ensemble number set to "Baby You Can Drive My Car."

Karla had to wake early in her tiny cabin (an inside room, no porthole, shared with Holly, the Second Female Vocalist), but she didn't mind getting up. On her narrow portion of desk, her music books—*The Best of Carole King, A Chorus Line, Godspell, Jesus Christ Superstar, Les Misérables, Little Shop of Horrors*—were lined up and alphabetized. Her mini-Casio was stashed under the bottom bunk, which Holly had claimed, and on it she could plunk out her parts for the Happy Sails Review. The Cruise Director had chosen Karla as featured soloist, which meant she would sing one song each week, any song she wanted, just as long as it was ship-appropriate—something familiar and upbeat, nothing with swearwords or overt religious references, which meant *Godspell* and *Jesus Christ Superstar* were out. She would get to rehearse with the band. She would wear her best and brightest dresses. She would have to think of a few lines of preceding witty repartee.

Each morning Karla slipped on her uniform and adjusted her name tag. She marched upstairs to the Main Deck to begin her day (Library Duty, followed by Mensa Hour) thinking of lyrics, thinking of opening lines. ("Good evening! Welcome aboard!" Would that be enough?) She marveled at where she was: *at sea.*

THE ENTERTAINERS were backed by the Tally-Ho Orchestra, which was not an orchestra, Karla discovered, but a four-piece band from Brighton. The guitarist sometimes kept a flask on his music stand. The drummer's bass drum had cracked weeks ago. "Humidity," he'd reported to the Cruise Director, when in fact the guitarist had done it, keeling over postshow. The drum had yet to be repaired.

The guitarist, Rod, admitted this quickly during Karla's very first band rehearsal for "I Feel the Earth Move," her upbeat choice. Rod drank from a tiny paper cup of coffee (free on the Pool Deck) and with his other hand thumped enthused Carole King rhythms on his blue-jeaned knee. Then they sat in silence and waited for the others to show up.

Karla counted the days since her arrival. *Only six?*

There were six ships in the Rodgers and Hammerstein fleet, one for each of the Rodgers and Hammerstein musicals made into films. Her ship (already she thought of it as hers), the MS *Sound of Music,* did the Canary Islands and the Western European itinerary—Barcelona, Nice, Naples—in homage to ecstatic singing from Alpine heights much farther inland. The winter Caribbean itinerary didn't have much to do with Julie Andrews at all.

Rod was out of coffee, so she asked him about the rest of the fleet.

The MS *State Fair* did the Eastern Mediterranean itinerary (he tried not to yawn)—Greece, Turkey, Israel, Egypt. This was the R and H movie musical no one had heard of, and, Greece aside, the Eastern Med was not the most popular destination for cruisers. So they were underappreciated jewels, both the show and the places.

Karla waited for him to crack a smile. He didn't.

The Persian Gulf itinerary went to the MS *Oklahoma.* "Persian Gulf" sounded better than "Middle East." *Oklahoma* (hokey, benign) was meant to put passengers at ease.

"That makes sense," said Karla, although it didn't.

The MS *King and I.* Pretty obvious: Far Eastern itinerary, including Thailand, Vietnam, and Hong Kong.

This one Karla had heard about from Holly. The Entertainers were required to sing "Getting to Know You" as each new batch of cruisers marched up the gangway.

"Poor sods," said Rod. Meaning the passengers, Karla guessed.

The MS *South Pacific* was another obvious one: South Pacific, featuring Bora-Bora and Tahiti.

And finally, the MS *Carousel.*

Here Karla took over: New York, New England, and Nova Scotia—the ship Karla's parents wished she'd been sent to, the one plowing through the cold, rough Atlantic. The movie had been filmed in her very own hometown in the fifties. Karla remembered the horrendous Maine accents and "A Real Nice Clambake," a song she knew well from her waitressing job. The MS *Carousel* was competitive, she told her folks. The Entertainers were recruited from New York, some between off-off-Broadway shows.

This information came out quickly. Rod gazed above her at the maroon stage curtains.

The others were called "sister ships," he concluded. Karla could see them in the shiny brochures at the Purser's Desk if she wanted. He peered again into his empty coffee cup.

The sister ships. Karla wondered if there was a way to jump from one to another—from the Med to the Middle East to Far East to South Pacific and then to Maine, the longest possible route home.

Then the orchestra showed up. The drummer carried a plastic tray of steaming paper cups. The keyboard player carried a handful of dairy creamers. The bassist yawned.

"Morning," said Rod, although it wasn't, and they nodded to him, then Karla, soberly.

KARLA MET THE ship duo, Zak and Macy, who hailed from the Isle of Wight and announced this nightly to guests. They called themselves Wight Nights and, like the rest of the musicians onboard, were free to play tourist by day as long as they were well-groomed and ready to go by dusk. Zak and Macy worked six nights per week, four hours per night, in the Anchor Lounge, the predinner set to the pre-DJ set. At 10:30 P.M., the Anchor became the Ship Disco. The rotating mirror ball descended, and the resident DJ, Mack, played the first of many Robbie Williams songs. The fog machine sprayed a fine chemical mist.

Before the ship gig, Wight Nights had played at hotels in Majorca and Tenerife—islands where Brits tended to gather, where the demand for pop songs was high, where the ability to sing in English was considered a worthy skill, they explained. (A *duo*. This was new to Karla, and she wanted to know as much as she possibly could.) They'd been at it for three years, four to six months in each place, leaving just before the expats became bored with them. If they were lucky, they had a few weeks off between gigs to see their parents, get their equipment repaired, and have their evening wear re-hemmed while their agent scrambled to find them the next job.

They'd see the world, the agent promised. The money was in the Middle East now—constant construction, new hotels every month. There was a circuit: Istanbul, Dubai, Muscat, Bahrain, and then, once you'd paid your dues, Tokyo and Bangkok and maybe Beijing or Seoul.

Bangkok! Beijing! Karla looked at Macy's photo albums and wanted, badly, to have her own pictures of the terra-cotta soldiers and the Great Wall.

She quizzed everyone: the fitness instructor, the head bartender, the photographers. She wanted to know how to make this last. She wanted to drift from one port to the next and the next without having to figure out why. She wanted things to happen *to* her.

✧

WITHIN KARLA'S FIRST three weeks onboard, she made out with the DJ and the Sous-Chef. The DJ made out with lots of people, men and women, he wasn't choosy. He could see that Karla was unsettled and new, and she could see that he had nicely sculpted arms and calves. She let him take off her uniform after her very first Daytime Darts Tourney, and there, in the locked DJ booth, he rubbed against her a little and was done. The next day he played "Let's Go Crazy" for her in the disco and then ducked out with a teenage boy from Devon. It didn't matter, Karla would say if asked, because there were so many other things to do.

No one asked.

The Sous-Chef did not make out with many. He had just divorced his wife of fifteen years, and he cried a lot. Karla stroked his hand in the crew bar and admired the silver tufts in his sideburns. Then they ate leftover tiramisu in his cabin. Before she could slip off her Evening Wear, he was sound asleep, his spoon resting on the white belly of his Ship Whites, making a small, chocolate smudge. Karla slid the spoon from his fist, licked it clean, and quietly returned to her cabin. One week later Sous flew home to Edinburgh. He asked for remarriage and the ex-wife said yes. Or so the story went in the crew bar.

KARLA MET THE VCAs, the Visiting Cabaret Acts, who entertained the passengers before and after the Happy Sails Review, the Hound Doggin' Review, and the Sing Along with Rodgers and Hammerstein Review. The Acts slept in passenger cabins and ate at the captain's table, but they partied with the crew. After performing, they didn't always want to socialize with the guests, who liked to tell them jokes of their own or sing renditions of "Yellow Rose of Texas." And so the Entertainers, Karla included, became unofficial hosts. They led the Acts through the maze of stairwells and cabins to the crew bar; they introduced them to the Russian waitresses; they told them where to buy joints in Grenada.

The Acts came for a few days at a time, which meant they arrived and departed from odd places. Spike the mime-magician boarded in Rome and left at Malta. George Jonesian, the U.K.'s number one country music artist, joined in Nice and flew home from Sardinia.

There were comedians—someone from Liverpool who'd once been a minor character on *Neighbours,* which was an Australian soap opera and not a Mister Rogers spin-off, as Karla had thought at first. There was the son of a game show host. There was a couple called MOON. (She danced in very small costumes, and he jumped into the audience and stole drinks from tables.) There was Sid the Canadian, who did a lot of "Have you ever noticed…" jokes, which Karla found amusing but no one else did. He had a gag about Canada offering all its bows and arrows whenever America went to war.

Because the comedians sometimes bombed, their turn-around tended to be particularly brief. Sid once joined in Lanzarote and left the next day from Fuerteventura, just twenty-three nautical miles away. Or so Karla had heard. It was a long way to come for one night, and she admired Sid the Canadian for this. He seemed as baffled and enchanted by the ship as she was. He slept through the early afternoon and drank his Earl Grey tea on the crew deck, staring down appreciatively at the churning water. Karla saw him there on the way to Shuffleboard, and he waved, shyly. She decided to be late for Shuffleboard.

"Tea," said Karla.

"Yes," said Sid. He smiled happily. He was cute in a bleached-out Californian way.

"Your first cruise?" she asked. It wasn't, of course, but he played along.

"Wonderful," he said. "The Midnight Buffet! And the entertainment is to die for." His accent was almost like hers. He dunked his tea bag and looked back at the waves.

She didn't see him after Shuffleboard, and then he was sent back to bleak and chilly Nova Scotia.

AFTER A MONTH onboard, Karla sang with Jack, an MS *Sound of Music* veteran of six months. He played a T-bird in the show, a Sea Bird in the ship version. He had only two speaking lines, and one was "Nice wheels, Mandy." That was all he'd said to Karla so far, but his British accent was delicious. He was twenty-nine.

The Cruise Director, Ava, told Karla and Jack to put something together for the predinner slot on Wight Nights' day off. Jack played guitar and Karla had "the jazzy thing," as Ava called it, confusing Karla's accent for an ability to mimic Ella Fitzgerald.

"Some standards," Ava suggested. "Something mellow." Something to keep the passengers drinking, she meant, as they waited for first seating.

Karla and Jack met in the empty Kiddie Room to rehearse. There were large cutouts of cartoon dolphins and turtles on the walls, and yellow buckets filled with Lego pieces. There was a wide-screen TV-VCR and a complete Disney video library. They sat side by side on bright red banquettes.

"Well," said Jack. He looked at a smiling dolphin as he spoke, and Karla studied him sideways. He smelled like a grown-up, like fresh limes and spices (Bay Rum), and his hair was dark and wavy. His acoustic guitar was polished, shiny, black.

Jack didn't know any standards, as it turned out, so they sang folky songs. Karla had brought her mellow songbooks (James Taylor, Joni Mitchell, Carole King), and he could follow, as long as she sang the melody clearly. She sang "So Far Away," and Jack clamped down his capo, and between them was a tangible buzz, an admission: *Yes, this person will do just fine.* Jack didn't cry or slink off with newlyweds—not yet, anyway— and Karla was grateful. They blended—they would learn to do it perfectly. Their voices would lock like Lego blocks, like the tiny silver buckles on Karla's size seven character shoes.

After six weeks, Karla still felt pleasantly frazzled. Her uniform didn't quite fit. Her pleated skirt was an inch too long, making her trip on stairs. The breast pocket of her blue blazer had pin marks from previous name tags. She was still understudying the *Hound Doggin'* part and had yet to perfect the blocking. The Dance Captain, who dated the real Captain, seemed forever busy and reluctant to rehearse. Karla was following, faking it. She was adept at faking. Beyond the Kiddie Room was Malta (Malta? Yes, Monday was Malta. Tuesday was Sardinia), all clay-colored and brilliantly hot, but this didn't concern Karla. There were such interesting things happening on the ship. She couldn't look away.

On Hoedown Night, Jack scooped her up and held her, petticoat showing, over the glistening pool. His cowboy hat tumbled in and quickly filled and sank, and the passengers hooted. "Put me down!" Karla shrieked, not meaning it, not wanting the burly sureness of him to disappear.

They went on dates in the passenger dining room, which they were allowed to enter if (A) the tables had empty seats and (B) they dressed up—suits and dresses—and wore name tags. They had to "PR" (speak affably) and not drink too much. They had to mention at least one entertainment option onboard that evening. But with Jack it was easy. "Good evening," he said, and instantly they were his, the couples from Bournemouth and Bromley and Slough. The questions were predictable: place of birth, trajectory onto the ship, musical training, favorite Broadway show, and Karla, part of the package, eventually charmed them, too.

"You don't really sound American," they said, and this pleased her. She'd taken him on, absorbed some of his tricks, the patterns of his speech. Her questions went down now, instead of up.

Karla had been dating someone named Arthur back in Boston, a composer from the New England Conservatory, but this ceased to concern her. She told herself this was a common ship phenomenon, the ship being a parallel but separate universe. It was something she couldn't possibly explain to anyone left behind. From time to time she felt an uncomfortable stab of guilt, usually when she spoke to her parents from the pay phone in Corsica. At those times the ship world seemed ridiculous—a bad prop, like the Pink Ladies car they danced around in *Hound Doggin'*. During rough seas it threatened to roll off its blocks and careen downstage.

Most of the time, however, Karla's parallel universe theory was convincing. The days were so long and the tiny bunks were like coffins and the need to have a body near was just, for both Karla and Jack, necessary. They soon left toothbrushes and lint pick-ups in each other's cabins, and their predinner set became a biweekly event. Their repertoire grew, and they received mild, distracted applause. They learned "Both Sides Now" and "You've Got a Friend." They added "Get Back" and "Under the Boardwalk" for contrast. Jack told a joke or two in between songs, and the passengers, who recognized him from Pool Deck quizzes and Ring Toss competitions, laughed politely.

Jack renewed his contract. Karla renewed, too, and together they sailed to the Caribbean. Arthur the Boyfriend stopped sending faxes to the bridge marked "Karla the Entertainer, Read This Please."

On days off, which they requested together, Jack and Karla ran on beaches, *Baywatch*-style, in snug, flattering swimsuits. There was sweet, fruity cocktail drinking and long, thorough sunblock rubbing and unread paperbacks from the Ship Library and a flurry of rushing to the gangway in time for duty.

At night, after the reviews, after the nightcaps in the crew bar, Karla slid into Jack's bunk and waited for him to floss. She kissed him sweetly until his roommate fell asleep and then kissed him less sweetly. Mornings she curled against his broad, solid back and wished for the Early Bird Quiz to be canceled. She began to feel an electric eel slipping around her chest, a spark in her belly. *This person will be more than fine.* For the first time in a while, Karla didn't want to be anywhere else.

"I like you very much," she said.

"I like you very much, too," he said.

They renewed again.

THE SHIP SEASONS changed again: winter in the Caribbean to spring in the Med, the long week at sea in between, the passengers fidgety, tired of shuffleboard. Karla wasn't frazzled anymore. She knew her parts and everyone else's. She kept her uniforms clean and pressed. She'd never missed a lifeboat drill, not one. She didn't whine to officials.

She whined privately, in the crew bar, and over gelati or tortillas or crepes in various Mediterranean cafés: The pay was too low, the costumes were worn, the duties were ridiculous (Monopoly Hour?), the cabins were claustrophobic, the crew mess was disgusting. They had to wear uniforms or dress up in all passenger areas, even on days off. They weren't allowed to sit on barstools or drink from bottles or cans in public. They had unannounced cabin inspections and curfews. And not a day passed without a minor drama within the Ents. Team: "You'll have to sing 'At the Hop.' Tonight." And Karla would panic and protest, and then do it.

She stayed because of Jack and because she was reminded, weekly, of Maine.

The MS *Sound of Music,* like all in the Rodgers and Hammerstein fleet, played a rotation of the sister ship musicals, one for each night of the week, plus *Love Boat* reruns on Sunday.

The films were shown in the Maria Lounge at midnight, an alternative to the disco or the casino. Nightly, Timmy the Sound and Light Guy closed the curtains, yanked down the cracked, white screen, and poured himself a generous whiskey and ginger in his booth. To keep himself amused, he tried to imagine the film stars naked—Yul Brynner and Deborah Kerr and Shirley Jones and Gordon MacRae. Yul was the easiest to imagine by far. (This Timmy admitted to Karla during a *King and I* viewing, after his third whiskey and ginger. Karla had been on Popcorn duty.)

Thursday was *Carousel* night, and each Thursday, Karla told the same story to passengers from Birmingham or Swansea or Portsmouth: *This was filmed right in my hometown, in Maine.*

"Does it still look like that?" they wanted to know.

It was difficult to say. She'd seen the film many times, but the only landmark she'd been able to catch was the Harbor Church. There were sailors with angled elbows and knees, hornpiping on a vast old dock, and there was the town church in the background, stark and white and nondescript. The rest just looked like sea.

"It was filmed such a long time ago," Karla said, by way of answer. But each week she made herself watch for a few minutes—it seemed wrong not to. Part of her hoped to catch something new, something recognizable that might make her feel homesick.

And then Timmy spilled a full pint of whiskey and ginger on the tape. It was beyond repair, and so the hornpipers were gone. Timmy was promptly docked twenty pounds from his paycheck. It would be months before Head Office would get around to sending a replacement copy.

Soon after, Jack made a suggestion on the crew deck, between the first and second shows. Karla was still in her poodle skirt. She was sitting on his lap, and the sun was setting deeply, with fire, over Malta. They were pulling away, the ship scraping and honking and rumbling, a cranky thing woken from a nap.

"We should become a duo," Jack said. He was not yet drunk—he was having one between-show vodka and Coke, as was customary.

She thought of the ship duos they had known since Wight Nights: Kiss and Tell and C-Note and Phantasy—they hardly spoke to each other. They had the dazed, worn quality of refugees. Most were alcoholics. They'd been doing this for six years, ten years, and they hated it. They had mortgages and equipment loans. They stole dinner rolls from the lunch buffet so they wouldn't have to buy food on land. They'd had to learn six hundred songs.

"They work four hours a day," Jack reminded her. "And we wouldn't be like that." He had an electric guitar in his parents' garage. Yes, they'd need equipment. Band stuff—amps and mike stands and speakers. A mixing board, a small one, and two microphones. But that was all. And songs, of course. They'd need lots and lots of songs.

Neither mentioned the other option. Their friends, Vic and Serena, both croupiers, were engaged. Vic bought the diamond on Saint Martin, where the prices were low. Mitch and Winnie, the ballroom dance instructors, were waiting on the rings but were planning to buy a small flat in Stevenage with their savings. Nick, the Second Male Vocalist, and Oliver, the Gift Shop Manager, had had a commitment ceremony in Barbados and would open a pub near Finsbury Park called

The Horny Toad. (Vic and Serena would last a month at home before returning to separate ships. Mitch and Winnie would have a baby boy within a year and move in with Mitch's parents. The Horny Toad would thrive.)

The sea rolled by, the land faded, the empty vodka glass rattled as it tipped and fell, then bumped across the deck. It didn't break, and so neither Karla nor Jack rose to retrieve it. Jack's lap was warm. Nothing stirred as Karla shifted her weight. He squeezed her ass a little, and the rest of the Team members milled around them like familiar guests.

"Okay," Karla said, fibbing. She knew she should have paused, thought it through, sought the advice of people back in the real world. She should have listened to the faint niggle of doubt buzzing inside.

But the air was salty, lovely. She was in her poodle skirt. She wanted, later, to spoon against his snug and sturdy back. "Sounds like a plan," she said.

They knew thirty-five songs between them.

ON JACK AND Karla's last night, Holly, who was still Karla's cabinmate, decorated the crew bar. The rest of the Entertainers, including Jack, were still cleaning up after Tropical Night—though Jack wasn't cleaning up per se. He was deep in conversation with Ava the Cruise Director—something about Tenerife. He'd squeezed Karla's knee distractedly and promised to be there soon.

Holly had arranged orange and pink balloons in clumps by the pool table and the pinball machine. The clump near the dartboard had already been destroyed. She bought Karla a gin and tonic and clinked glasses and hugged her tightly. Then she left to play pool with the new Estonian masseur.

Sid the Canadian was back, slumped on a barstool and drinking tequila. He'd just done a late-night show in the Maria Lounge.

"Where have you been?" said Karla.

"Freezing my ass off," said Sid. "Rotarian banquet in Portland. Convention for orthodontists in Halifax. (They can *drink*. You wouldn't think so.) A bachelor party for a very distant cousin. Should I go on?"

"You're a Brit, technically," Karla said, sitting beside him. "Or something in between a Brit and a Yank." She wouldn't have said it, normally—she knew Canadians were touchy about these things—but he seemed in need of distraction. She meant he could cross British borders without too much hassle.

Sid blinked at her. His hair was spiky and still very blond, despite the winter back home. He didn't have laugh lines yet, she noticed—odd for a comedian—and his chin had an off-center indent, something she hadn't seen before, as though he'd been bitten there as a child. His face drooped a little from tequila.

"I'm not a funny person, am I?" he said. He flicked a small section of lime off the bar, and it landed on Karla's lap, mottled and brownish.

The Sous-Chef had asked something similar before he fell asleep with the tiramisu spoon. There was no correct response. *I think you're funny* or *What is funny?* were either too lame or too out there. She bought Sid a shot instead.

"My parents were—are—Scottish. So I'm Scottish, I guess. Of Scottish descent. To answer your nationality question." He sipped.

"It wasn't a question, really." Karla sipped.

"Or comment. Whatever." He smiled a little, finally.

"I like your bow and arrow joke," Karla offered.

"Thanks. It never gets a laugh."

This was *banter*, Karla realized, and with Sid she could do it, this volleying of replies, back and forth. She was usually not so good at it, not with Brits. They lobbed their responses too quickly, and their references were cryptic. With Sid the pace was fine, and she knew exactly what he was talking about: Maine and Nova Scotia and skiing versus staying in the ski lodge to drink and how lobster bisque was a complete waste of a lobster.

She waited for a lull. "You know we're leaving tomorrow, Jack and I."

"Day off?"

"Our contract's over. We're going to be a duo."

"Wow." Sid let this sit with him for a while. "Are you worried?"

"Wow," she echoed. Maybe this was unique to North Americans, to point to the very thing that gnawed, to force it into conversation.

"I *am* worried," she said, "a little," and something lifted. She twisted on her stool to see if Jack had returned, if he had sensed her honesty spilling out four decks below. No one there but Sid.

"Maybe I'll join you," he said. "Maybe I'll be in the duo too."

"Sure, come along," she said.

"Where's your first gig?" He seemed slightly more sober now, despite the shot. He seemed determined to remember this information.

"We don't have one. We're going to England first, before we get our gigs."

"What if you don't get your gigs? *Gigs. Gigs. Gigs.* One of those words that means nothing with repetition."

"We'll get gigs. Jobs. We'll get work." They *would*.

"The sister ships," he said, and Karla knew he was changing the subject for her, steering her away from too much truth.

And then he tumbled from the barstool and landed hard on the beer-stained carpet. Holly laughed and the Estonian frowned and the Filipino guys looked up from their cribbage game briefly. Sid hoisted himself up by gripping Karla's thigh. It was a startling clench, pinching straight through her Evening Wear skirt. She liked it. There would be a bruise if he kept at it, something she'd have to hide from Jack.

Sid turned to look for Jack himself, removed his hand, and then continued. "The sister ships. I want to see them. If you're an Act, sometimes you can do a world tour, a week on each ship."

"*If* you're an Act. Lucky."

Holly winked at Karla from across the bar, and Karla pretended not to see.

"So when are you going?" Karla asked him. "When does the world tour begin?"

"Oh, they haven't offered yet, not officially. Not when I keep bombing. Speaking of which."

Jack strolled in then, with the Entertainment Team in tow. He scanned the room and rested his very green eyes on Karla, then Sid.

"Sid Vicious," said Jack. "What are you drinking?" Then he grabbed Karla's thigh in the very same spot.

KARLA AND JACK departed from Aruba the next day, and at the gangway a few friends gathered, surprisingly few. Ava was absent, but Roger, the Assistant Cruise Director, shook their hands and gave them shiny MS *Sound of Music* pins to keep. Marcie from the Purser's Desk, who'd had a brief pre-Karla fling with Jack, cried quietly. Vic, Serena, Mitch, Winnie, Nick, and Oliver held hands. They'd seen this in a musical somewhere, a similar departure.

"He may never ask you, sweetie," Serena whispered to Karla. "You know that."

"Maybe she doesn't want to be asked," said Winnie.

"Everyone likes to be asked," said Oliver.

The Teamsters waved and shouted out private jokes Karla would soon forget. Then they smoothed their blazers and returned to their duties: bingo and ballroom dance lessons and darts.

Sid didn't show. Neither did Holly, who'd slipped out of the crew bar with the Estonian.

And just like that, it was sucked away from Karla—the sun and the geckos and that neat pizza place in Oranjestad— and there they were, moving on to something unknown. On the plane, Jack slept and Karla was glad, though she kept holding his hand. She wondered if, away from loud and animated people, they'd have less to say. But a complimentary Baileys on ice arrived, and this thought was postponed. Karla gently released Jack's hand.

They landed in York, England, where Jack's parents lived, where they would borrow an apartment from Jack's school friend, who was traveling in Australia; he'd always had a thing for Kylie Minogue, Jack explained. They'd stay there until they'd recorded a demo tape and signed a contract, which wouldn't take long—one month, two? They had savings, and Jack had another buddy who'd help them record the demo for nothing. It was March. By May they'd be out of there. June at the latest.

York turned various shades of gray: charcoal, steel, ashen. Karla lost her tan. She met Jack's parents, who'd never known a half-Jewish person before.

"We eat bagels all the time," his mom said.

In the apartment Karla took down the Kylie poster above the bed. She could hear the customers in the sandwich shop below and smell salty whiffs of sausage rolls and shepherd's pies. She bought garbage bags and bread and newspapers for the first time in over a year. She cleaned the tiny bathroom and did the laundry. And she learned songs, at least three per week. She kept a blank tape in the boom box and left the radio on. When she heard a good one, she rushed across the room and pressed Record and scribbled the lyrics on a yellow legal pad. She memorized verses and choruses as she walked to Shoppe and Go for groceries and to Fitness Palladium for aerobics classes.

They made their demo tape. The vocals were too low, and Jack's guitar solos were too long, but Karla sent it out anyway, to every ad in *The Stage* for "girl-boy hi-tech duos." She included a picture from the *Sound of Music*—arms linked, smiling in their formal wear. (The ship pho-togs had printed one hundred copies for nothing and let them keep the negatives.) Karla followed up; she called the London numbers and left dignified messages in an accent that, her mother said, was becoming less and less American.

Jack, meanwhile, borrowed his father's car and drove to

Newcastle to check on equipment prices. He played soccer with his school friends. He spent entire evenings in the pub playing pool. Karla was welcome to join them, he said, but she probably wouldn't have a good time.

"Back by eleven," he promised, and kissed her carefully on the lips.

The eel flicked its long electric tail in Karla's belly.

Spring passed, and Jack was offered a summer singing job by Ava the Cruise Director. It was a "fly back" deal, in family-style hotels in the Canary Islands. He would spend one week there and one week back in York. He would be a Visiting Cabaret Act.

"That's a laugh," he said, but Karla knew he was pleased. He pulled out his Sinatra records and bought an expensive sport jacket the color of limes. He learned "Cat's in the Cradle" and "Let Me Entertain You" and "Hello" by Lionel Richie (Karla's suggestion). He practiced in the living room, telling jokes he'd heard on the ship, singing in a way that was sweet and manly. Ava had recognized this, Jack's earnest appeal, and it was why she'd recommended him so highly, Karla knew. The VCA job paid well, and it was just until they got the duo thing sorted out.

Of course he should take it, Karla said.

It was June. By August they'd be out of there, he said, September at the latest.

She went with him once, but the prop planes between the islands made her nervous and she had no one to sit with during the shows. Afterward, large potbellied men with pints of beer swarmed around Jack. They had jokes of their own to tell. They had versions of "Cat's in the Cradle" to deliver.

"Can't we leave?" she whispered. "Take a walk on the beach, alone?"

But Jack was impossibly polite and charming to all. He already knew everyone—the bartenders, the pool guys. He knew the receptionist and the fitness instructor and the bartender, who all touched him on the arm when they spoke.

"They seem like good service-industry girls," Karla said, despite herself.

"And boys," said Jack.

"And boys."

In Tenerife they missed the MS *Sound of Music* by one day, just one stop too late. Karla had wanted, badly, to see the Entertainers again.

AND SO KARLA didn't fly out with Jack again. Back in York she was invited to do things with Jack's cousin Raquel, who lived in Newcastle and smoked heavily and liked shopping. Karla went along with her twice to the enormous Newcastle Mall to look at jewelry and towel sets and cargo pants. She began to tell the cousin she was busy—she had songs to learn. Raquel didn't press her for details.

She went to Break-Away Travel, where there were racks of catalogs for cruise lines, a whole wall of competing itineraries. In the MS *Sound of Music* brochure, she flipped to page 22, under "Schnitzel with Noodles and More! Your Fine Dining Options," and found herself, champagne flute tipped toward Jack's, the Photoshop-enhanced sky gleaming Kool-Aid grape behind their heads. The photographer had said, "Snuggle closer! Give her a snog!" And Karla and Jack had laughed and kissed deeply and tried to look lovelier.

Karla dropped the brochure on the Break-Away counter and let it fall open to the schnitzel page. "How *are* the dining options on this one?" she asked.

"I haven't been," said CHERYL, eyes fixed on her computer screen, fingers flying. Her name tag was crooked, and Karla wanted to yank it straight. "Take the brochure, if you want," she said, when Karla didn't leave. "We have tons."

She took the brochure. In the flat she ripped out the schnitzel page carefully and stuck it under a Kylie Minogue fridge magnet. Jack would say, "I was skinnier then," which was true, and Karla would say, "At least it was real champagne." The photographer had given them the option, ginger ale or the real stuff, and of course they hadn't needed to consult.

JACK RETURNED from the Canaries late on Sundays and wanted to eat, drink, canoodle, and sleep, in that order. To pass the time on Sunday afternoons, Karla bought the *Guardian* and the *Independent* and read everything, even the Sainsbury's coupons and the clearance sale promos for Woolworths.

On this particular Sunday in late July, it was after eight when she finally made it to "Travel" (she'd saved it for last) and a tiny blurb on page nine caught her eye: CANADIAN JUMPS SHIP IN IBIZA.

KARLA WAITED until Jack smeared his vindaloo grease with the last piece of naan. She'd already asked him about his trip. (Tiring. Good. Someone had mistaken him for Gary Barlow. He'd figured out what airports smell like: cardboard.)

"I found something in the paper," said Karla, taking his plate. "About Sid."

"Hm," said Jack. He looked sleepy and sore. "Sid who?"

"Sid the comedian. Canadian. He jumped in Ibiza."

Jack focused then. He sat up a little. "What—jumped over?"

"Jumped ship—left. Just didn't come back to the gangway in time and the ship had to leave without him. He's missing. I read it in the paper."

"That's news? He probably just got pissed in Ibiza and didn't make it back."

"He 'disappeared,' it said."

"He didn't want to bomb again. He was kind of a shuck, wasn't he?"

Karla waited for him to explain.

"He was a shuck, as you would say."

"*Schmuck. Shuck* is something you do with clams."

"I wouldn't know about that either, Maine girl." He smiled and made a grab for her, but she wasn't ready for that yet.

"People don't do that—leave the ship."

"Sure they do. He got drunk, he missed the ship, he watched it pull away and thought, *Fuck.* He didn't have his cell phone so he couldn't ring the bridge and ask them to turn around. Not that our fine Captain would waste fuel on one bad Act."

"He probably didn't have his passport with him."

"He could go to the embassy."

"He wouldn't know where to find it."

"He could ask someone. Why do you care?"

Why did she care?

"How many times did you think about jumping yourself," said Jack, "just staying on your ass in the café or wherever and watching the fucker pull away without you? It would be lovely, a vodka-Coke and a fag and the beast disappearing. Instead of calling in sick, the job leaves you. It's the perfect excuse."

"But we never did it," Karla said, "because it would be awful once we finished our drinks. We'd have to pay for food and a hotel, and we wouldn't have our passports."

"We could go to the embassy. We've been over this."

Karla wondered about the opposite of jumping ship—stowing away, refusing to leave rather than refusing to stay. But she didn't think Sid was the stowaway type. He'd have no audience, for one.

Jack picked up a section, "Science and Technology," which meant the discussion was over. They watched TV, and he fell asleep on the couch with his head tipped against her chest. His hair smelled just like cardboard.

JACK WAS IN Gran Canaria again when the phone rang. It was 11:30 A.M. on an August Tuesday, and Karla had just finished her second cup of tea. She was humming the chorus to "Stand by Me" and wondering if it was really necessary to buy a new bottle of Woolite, and then she was speaking to a woman named Liza, an agent, who wanted to send them to Abu Dhabi for three months.

Liza was a former chef with good hotel contacts. (She threw this in quickly, to get it off her chest.) She was sixty-five and smoked menthols, Karla deduced.

"And your Jack can actually play that guitar of his?" Liza asked.

"Of course."

"And you can do four forty-fives?"

They could do four forty-fives for one night, yes. They'd need to add five more nights of songs.

"No problem."

"And your name, Northern Lights. That's official?"

"Yes," Karla said. "We're Northern Lights."

"It's a TV show, right? In America?"

"That's *Northern Exposure*," said Karla.

"Fine then," said Liza. "Four forty-fives. Meals and flights and one room, shared. Freight expenses paid for."

"Fine," said Karla.

She hung up and squealed in the empty flat. She scanned the one poster she'd tacked to the living room wall, "The Map of the World." It took a few minutes, but she found it. Abu Dhabi. It was pink, and tiny, and blessedly far away. They'd leave in two weeks.

She was a singer again.

PINK SEEMED APT. Abu Dhabi, Karla read, was all "searing sun" and drunk expats. There were shiny office towers and tall hotels, with miles and miles of sand beyond. "Miami without the lox. Miami with Sahara creeping in." In the hotels drinking was legal, and so all hotels had bars. In the bars there were musicians. This Karla read in her first Lonely Planet guide: The United Arab Emirates. It was much thinner than the other Lonely Planets. The cover showed a surly camel and a clay-baked wind tower.

JACK HAD TO CUT the cabaret gig short, and Nick from The Horny Toad took his place. Oliver would stay at home and mind the pub.

Jack began to learn guitar parts, fast. The living room was scattered with songbooks from the York Public Library: *100 Great Country Tunes, The Best Pop Songs Ever, Soul Train Hits, The Complete Eagles Anthology.*

Karla tested him for lyrics.

"Verse two, 'Lyin' Eyes'—go."

"Another night, it's gonna be a strong one—"

"*Long* one. How could it be a 'strong' one?"

"Strong one—a strong night, a good night."

"She's leaving him—how can it be a good night?"

"Oh, fuck—write it down."

So she wrote out "Lyin' Eyes" in block letters and added it to his alphabetized folder, to be propped on a music stand. "For practice. You can't use this onstage."

But he would, and they both knew it. He would smile and twinkle, and no one but Karla would care what words he sang.

They packed. Karla bought four kinds of sunscreen and three pairs of sandals. Jack had his lime jacket dry-cleaned and pressed. He packed it carefully, right on top.

TWO

Northern Lights

Abu Dhabi, United Arab Emirates, 1996

At the Abu Dhabi airport, a glass wall stood between the bleary passengers, Jack and Karla among them, and the place they hoped to enter. Pressed close to the glass was a throng of robed men, gesturing wildly, throwing their hands forward as if to say, *Go away!*

"What are they doing?" Karla said. "Being friendly?"

Karla and Jack would soon understand that the gesture actually meant *Hey, come here—come to me,* just as they would soon know that these were not Emirati men but lackeys for Emiratis, sent to retrieve arriving guests. They were Indians and Pakistanis and Bangladeshis. They wore kurtas of pastel blues and oranges, of very light greens and browns, rather than the Emiratis' required white robes.

Karla filled out her entry form (Occupation: Entertainer. Religion: Methodist) and waited in line with Jack. At the customs desk their passports were examined by a white-robe, who scrawled a line of Arabic under the necessary stamp. They showed him their contract, faxed from the hotel.

"You will need to make the bimonthly visa run," said the man, with a hint of a London accent.

"Excuse me?" said Karla. "Visa what?"

"Fine, yes," said Jack. "Thank you very much." He gathered their papers and steered Karla away.

"We'll ask later," he said, and they made their way to baggage. Beyond the gesturing men were women in black, some with their faces covered, some with gold ornaments hooked over their noses and foreheads. There were a few falcons in cages. There were palm trees inside, potted in gold urns the size of washing machines.

A gesturing man found them quickly and introduced himself as Hamad. He wore a name tag and a tan uniform. "Welcome to the fine, hot weather, yes?" His mustache was full, and he smelled of starch. He carried their bags to the gleaming hotel van in the parking lot.

They were in.

Karla got through because her last name wasn't Jewish-sounding. This was why Liza had inquired about her name, casually, in a follow-up phone call. "Tell me your last name again," she'd said. "And spell it, please."

Liza had had trouble once with a pianist called Bernie James, she later told Karla and Jack. Bernie's real name, the name in his passport, was James Bernstein. Bernie arrived, went to the UAE customs desk, and was sent back to Heathrow on the next available flight.

Karla's parents probably wouldn't be allowed to visit. They'd been to Israel; the stamp was in their passports to prove it.

"Take notes," her father had said. "And don't go to Mc-Donald's." She should stay close to Jack at all times, and she shouldn't speak loudly in public places—in fact, she should adopt a British accent.

"The sun," said Jack now, to Hamad.

"Yes, it is hot," Hamad agreed.

This was September, Hamad reminded them, the hottest time of the year. The flat, khaki desert receded behind, and the city center appeared—a dozen tall, sparkling towers clustered ahead. "And, by the way, your equipment is here now also," said Hamad. They would start the following night.

"We used to work on a cruise ship," Jack told Hamad. "We met there, as singers." He looked at Karla, realizing how bizarre it sounded. *We're new to this,* he meant, *this duo thing.*

Hamad nodded slowly and steered them into the sun.

✧

IN BAR BLUE, on their very first night of work, a small Indian man was propped against the wall, directly under the dartboard. He'd arrived just after noon, when the bar opened. Karla saw him on her way back from the lunch buffet, which Jack had skipped. By the time they began their first set, at 8:00 P.M., the man was nearly catatonic. He blinked and smiled a little as Karla took out her shiny, new tambourine.

"It will pick up," said Zahid, the Bar Manager. "They go home for the hot time, the England guys. But they'll be back soon." Zahid wore a pin-striped vest and a bow tie, the Bar Blue uniform. His hair was pure white; he was fifty-three years old, he said.

The Food and Beverage Manager soon joined them. (Rotund, rumpled, Syrian. He'd known Liza for twenty-two years.) He shook Jack's hand and welcomed them to "the best bar in Abu Dhabi." He requested "Private Dancer," which they didn't know.

Karla and Jack played on a low corner stage with a large TV set bolted close to their left speaker. The bar was small and cozy, pub-style, but the decor was all wrong—yellows and blues, Formica tables, carpets that were too clean and too new. Karla, that first night, wore her favorite Formal Night dress, the one she'd worn weekly to the Captain's Ball: red, clingy, tiny balletic threads grazing her shoulders, sheer satiny material down to her toes. Red was her color, she knew. But the dress was too much for the bar—she sensed this instantly, as Zahid gawked and F and B frowned.

"Princess Diana!" said the Indian man.

IN THE MORNINGS they watched *Le Grind* on MTV and saw women with actual body parts: bellies and shoulders and thighs. Karla didn't bother unpacking her shorts and tank tops. She wore the same pair of long, white pants every day, and a little shawl she bought in the gift shop. Lonely Planet insisted it was perfectly acceptable for Westerners to expose legs and arms "within reason," but it didn't feel acceptable to Karla, at least not in the streets.

THEY WOULD HAVE to do quizzes, F and B informed them. The Quiz Night was quite popular with the England guys, he said, and they gave good prizes—a camera, a radio, three pitchers of beer.

In their room, Karla protested. Too shiplike, she said. They'd done that already.

"It's not a big deal," Jack said. "Twenty questions. We can come up with twenty questions a week, surely."

She'd have to come up with the questions, she knew, and he'd read them out, telling jokes in between, milking the mike. She'd hand out pencils and paper and do the scoring and present the prizes.

"I hate quizzes," Karla said. She believed in "onward and upward." She'd done her daytime duties, and now she wanted range and strength. This was bound to happen, she reasoned, singing four forty-fives per night. She would be both a belter and a crooner. She would be Patsy Cline and Cher, Aretha Franklin and Joni Mitchell. She would develop a big voice, a sensitive voice, a voice that would cause people to say, "What is she doing *here*?"

She believed this to be possible. The quizzes would distract her, she said to Jack, from learning all her lyrics, from practicing.

"Forgive me, Ms. Houston," he said.

She was getting irritated by this tactic. Constant jokes— mean jokes sometimes, covered up with smiles and winks and nudges. She considered her options for a second or two: play along or strike back.

"You can call me Whitney," Karla made herself say. And together they descended for the lunch buffet by the pool.

KARLA HAD TO make bimonthly trips on her own to renew her visa, just as the customs man in white had warned. It was easy—a twenty-minute flight to the nearest non-Emirati airport, in Doha, Qatar. (And once, when this flight was booked, to Kish Island, Iran.) When she came back to Abu Dhabi each time, she received another two-week tourist stamp.

She complained to Liza, by phone.

"Think of it as free travel," said Liza.

"To Doha?"

Jack, meanwhile, was fine. As a citizen of the Commonwealth, he could come and go as he pleased.

"One of the benefits of colonialism," he said.

"This hasn't been one of yours for a while," Karla corrected. "They just need you now to do their oil digging."

"I believe we call them engineers," he said. "Enjoy your flight."

KARLA WANTED TO visit a mosque. She asked Zahid.

"Not allowed," he said, stirring grenadine into her ginger ale. "You are not permitted inside, Miss Karla."

Neither was Jack. All that pained singing five times a day, the voices blasting out from pretty spires, and they couldn't even have a peek. After three weeks, they still hadn't met one real local, although there were Emirati men everywhere—pacing the streets, the mall, their white robes swishing, expensive sandals and watches flashing out from underneath. They cocked their heads to speak into their cell phones and drove spotless Jeep Cherokees (the perfect vehicles for weekend "dune bashing"), taking up two spaces in parking lots. If you'd been born there, you didn't have to work, Zahid explained.

"What do they all do, exactly?" Karla asked.

"Government positions," Zahid said. "Board members. Very important jobs."

"Figureheads," said Jack. She waited for him to wink. He winked.

"HOW OFTEN DO cruise ships come?" Karla asked Zahid.

"We have *Kitty Hawk* sometimes," said Zahid. "Not here— Abu Dhabi is too small for the big ships—but in Dubai, the next Emirate over. In Dubai, during the Gulf War, all the sailors came out—the bars were very busy then. Party time."

Kitty Hawk? For a moment Karla forgot what this was. One of Carnival's?

"Military," Zahid reminded her. He used three syllables instead of four.

"Oh yes," said Karla. "Navy. We worked on a cruise ship."

"I know," said Zahid. *"The Love Boat."*

"Exactly," said Karla.

THEIR DAYS WERE still filled with song learning and set organizing and quiz planning. Karla hunted for trivia online, having already run through all the Pool Deck questions she could remember, the largest and fastest and smallest questions— animals, countries, athletes. They were up to ninety-seven songs, which meant they still had to repeat too many songs per week, which meant they still had to practice every day.

And then one afternoon, while they were rehearsing in the bar, a local walked in. He looked familiar to Karla— something about the shape of his beard and his calm, certain manner. He was followed by five other solemn men in red and white checkered head scarves. F and B seemed to be giving them a tour.

"Hello," said calm eyes. "Good day. I see you are musicians."

"We try," said Jack.

"I am a fan of country music. Kenny Rogers: 'Coward of the County.' Willie Nelson: 'On the Road Again.'" It was unclear whether these were requests or observations.

"Great songs," said Karla. How did she know him?

"From America and Britain," F and B explained.

"Welcome," said the man, just short of smiling, and turned to go.

"I know him," said Karla.

"I doubt it," said Jack. "He's the sheikh of Dubai."

"How do I know what he looks like?"

"That's him, everywhere." He meant the portraits in all hotel lobbies, on billboards, the standard photo used in all *Gulf News* articles: stately, official, frozen in perfectly flattering light.

EXACTLY ONE WEEK later Zahid had to escort another Emirati—not the sheikh—away from the bar entrance. "Sorry, sir," Zahid said, steering without touching. "We serve alcohol here. Perhaps you'd like to relax in our lobby café?"

"Kar," said Jack, whispering off mike. "This is a good one: 'They're not allowed in our places of worship either.'"

"Don't you dare say it," she whispered back. She felt a pang for him then, like kissing secretly on the Promenade Deck after curfew. They were allies. They would stick together or be damned.

Eventually, the expats returned (red-faced, beer-bellied English lads, age twenty-five to twenty-eight, Karla guessed). They sat in front. Karla and Jack were in the middle of "Scarborough Fair" when one rose to push up the volume on the TV (rugby—Ireland versus Australia).

Karla nearly pounced. Jack quickly skipped a verse and a chorus and said they'd be back in fifteen, which would be twenty, and led her to the bar.

"Leave it," he said. "It doesn't matter." She opened her mouth, and he beat her to it. "We work here. We're the worker bees." He ordered a gin and tonic for her and a vodka and Coke for himself.

"They weren't listening."

"They're not here to listen." He left off "to you," and she was grateful for this.

She sipped, and the gin tang hit her throat and began to do its good work and soon she felt better.

✧

KARLA DEVELOPED A cough. It was the air-conditioning and the smoke, she supposed, and the nightly hours of singing. Jack sympathized and headed downstairs to do the sets on his own, plus the weekly quiz.

The next night Karla put on a brave face, and Zahid plied her with Magic Mixture, a blend of hot water, lemon, honey, and cognac. She thanked him—it was lovely.

"You are most welcome, Miss Karla. I will take care of you." He gave her a brusque, official pat on the shoulder. He said she shouldn't drink cold things. Ever. He said it was very good she'd decided to work tonight—the bar was much better with a lady for them to look at. And, by the way, their pay would be docked next time she didn't show.

They began to know the regulars. There was Elvis (with sideburns) from Wales, who could hardly speak by the time they started work, and who insisted on buying Jack full pints even when he asked for halves. There was orange-haired Bea from New Zealand, who sat alone, and who also appeared to be an alcoholic. The Turkish architect with the mustache stood when they entered the bar and said, "I am an architect." The skinny French man with funny teeth said, *"Bon soir,"* to which they replied, *"Bon soir,"* to which he then added, "I am French." And on and on through *"Comment allez-vous?"* and *"ça va bien"* and more toothy smiles, and much shoulder squeezing. And the lads up front began to take notice. They were geologists, assessing Emirati ground for oil. When they liked a song (Rod Stewart, Rolling Stones), they clapped along with the entire wingspans of their arms.

Jack and Karla began to get requests, mostly for "Hotel California," which they were happy to do because it was six minutes long. The requests were scrawled on bits of napkin ("Please, 'Pink Champagne on Ice' song for Mohammed"), and the waitresses delivered the scraps to the stage, to Karla, because her hands were free, except when she chose to experiment with her tambourine. The more the regulars drank, the more they requested. The more they requested, the more songs Karla and Jack had to learn. But they needed new songs, and it was good for them, having to learn quickly and fake it, like ship days. Jack's fingers had calluses, and Karla's range was expanding, bit by bit. She lost the cough quickly. She could do "If I Could Turn Back Time" by Cher without cracking.

ZAHID DECORATED the bar with holly and tinsel for the English guys. Ramadan was approaching, and Jack and Karla's contract would soon end. The foreign musicians weren't allowed to perform for the month, and so most went home.

Why hang out and not eat in public for thirty days? Karla heard stories from the regulars. You couldn't chew gum. You couldn't be seen smoking. But it wasn't as torturous as it sounded. There were tents set up outside, next to all the hotel swimming pools. At sundown the party began, and the locals ate and ate, stuffing themselves to make it through the next twelve hours. It was a kind of Mardi Gras without the booze.

Still, Karla and Jack opted to leave. Liza hadn't yet mentioned another job.

Zahid served free, cheap champagne on their last night, and the Turkish architect made a toast that no one understood.

The equipment might have to remain for a week or two longer than expected, Liza reported. Was that okay? Ramadan and all, business was not as usual, not quite up to speed.

Fine, Jack and Karla said. They didn't plan on playing a note during their break.

They packed and flew back to York, to drizzle. They hadn't seen rain in three months. Jack's parents had a large Christmas tree, and their presents were waiting underneath.

On the fifth day in York, Jack's cell phone rang. They were in the pub, playing pool. Or Jack played pool as Karla ate a Wispa and watched. He handed the phone over so he could shoot.

They'd been asked back, said Liza. Abu Dhabi again. Just three quick months and then she'd find them something new. Karla felt a sinking inside. They knew Abu Dhabi—it would be more of the same. Hot days by the pool and the same weird French guy and glasses of Magic Mixture.

"Again?" said Karla. Jack missed the shot, and she went outside to finish the call. The pub overlooked York's famous church, York Minster. Medieval, important-looking—she hadn't been there yet.

"They loved you there," Liza insisted, "especially on Quiz Nights." The Bar Blue patrons had rallied to hire them back. Mohammed, who won the quiz weekly, had given them a very strong recommendation. (He had, no doubt, treated the Food and Beverage Manager to a lunch of whiskey shots and called Jack and Karla "genuine trivia experts" and "musically versatile." What were they called again? Northern Lights, that was it. Northern Lights. Mohammed thought they should stay.)

"They want you back," Liza insisted. It was a nice thought, but Karla knew it wasn't entirely true. The expats wanted fresh blood, new versions of "Hotel California." Liza just hadn't been able to find anyone to replace them.

After Eid, when the poolside tents came down and the fasting was over, they'd be allowed to return, Liza said. And after that, Asia. It was sorted.

BUT AFTER ANOTHER three months in Abu Dhabi (Mohammed finally lost a quiz; the geologists chipped in and bought Karla a new tambourine), they were sent to Dubai, just two hours up Sheikh Zayed Road. It was just like Abu Dhabi, only bigger, glitzier. There were more shopping malls, more beaches, more Jeep Cherokees, more hotels. There was a Planet Hollywood and a Hard Rock Cafe. In Dubai, bands were sometimes flown in from the U.S. Maybe Karla wouldn't feel quite so outnumbered there, so completely surrounded by citizens of the Commonwealth.

Jack decided he liked the Emirates, Dubai in particular. He bought a secondhand Mercedes for two thousand dollars and asked Karla to take pictures of him beside it, with the aqua-green Gulf in the background. He invited his parents out, and the school friend, who was on his way back from Australia and had to be reminded not to carry his beer outside.

For a while they took daily trips to the beach. The Merc ran well and gas was cheap and the roads were clear. They went early, before the heat set in—the goal was to be in the ocean by nine o'clock sharp. (They could always take an afternoon nap.) They bought magazines on the way, and cans of Orange Crush. They sprawled on hotel towels and read about Posh and Becks in glossy issues of *Hello!*

By ten, the beach was crowded. A few Indian women swam fully clothed; the rest were shirtless Emirati boys, their new Jeeps parked only feet from the shore.

Karla and Jack sat close to the water, and Jack dribbled wet sand on Karla's legs. With gritty fingers he swept a strand of hair away from her eyes.

"You're looking awfully brown," he said.

"Thank you," said Karla.

They were good like this, on beaches, in water. They could pretend they were on the ship somewhere in the Caribbean, that they had a different life to rush back to, someone else's schedule to follow, a curfew to obey.

"Nice wheels, Mandy," Jack said, in his worst American accent.

She kissed him sweetly, as *Hound Doggin'* Mandy would.

There were jellyfish, and once Karla got stung. Jack went running and a few times convinced Karla to join him. The sand made her feet raw, and her calves ached pleasingly, later.

And then they stopped. They were too tired to get up or Jack was too hungover to drive. Karla developed a sun rash.

There was nothing on the horizon in the way of vessels, just a flat line of sea.

✦

KARLA LINGERED in Web Kingdom, Dubai's largest Internet café, which was cool and dim inside. She looked up "Dubai Ship Terminal," which had 103 berths for dry goods and big containers and other trade-related things. And cruise ships.

The ship terminals Karla had seen had varied in terms of appeal. In Civitavecchia, the port closest to Rome, passengers were greeted by a large, metallic warehouse and dazed, shirtless men on cranes. In Martinique there was a lone boy selling canned pineapple juice from a cooler. Saint Martin had no official berths at all, but because semiprecious stones were still cheap there, the *Sound of Music* "tendered," or anchored itself offshore. The pax were untenderly ferried to shore in the ship's cramped lifeboats and returned with bangles, pendants, toe rings, chokers.

The Dubai Ship Terminal, by contrast, looked like an enormous bank: white pillars and wide driveways, freshly tarred. The Web site pictures were clear and sharp and taken from flattering angles. Karla could see a food court, a post office, a duty-free shop for cigarettes and perfume and medicinal rows of rum and gin. (The Dubai Ship Terminal was in a tax-free zone, ungoverned by Sharia law, Karla read.) There was a row of silver, gleaming ATMs, and a fenced exhibit of Emirati things: a camel carved from teak, a coffee tent for shade in the desert sun, a golden coffee urn, a fishing net, a pile of oysters. A gleaming pearl necklace inside a glass case.

You could live inside this ship terminal if you had to. You could jump the exhibit's barricade and curl up in the coffee tent at night; you could wake to falafel or curry or stir-fry. You could pay your bills and mail your postcards and treat yourself to a duty-free nightcap of Baileys or Kahlúa. Or you could just run your errands and return to the ship outside. You could walk from one self-contained life to another.

Karla wanted to see the Dubai Ship Terminal in person, just to touch the coffee tent and the shiny urn.

But then Liza called again.

FROM DUBAI THEY were sent to Doha, Qatar (the city turned out to be just as enticing as the airport Karla knew well), and from Doha they went to Muscat, Oman (fewer high-rises, more camels and clay-colored wind towers). They were seeing the world, Liza reminded them, the Muslim world.

Two other duos—Milk and Honey from Liverpool and Double Speak from Cape Town—were working in Muscat, and they forged an alliance. On their day off (Friday, the holy day), they packed a Styrofoam cooler with ice and stolen buffet sandwiches and piled into a borrowed Jeep to see the dunes. Or they drank cocktails at one of their pool bars and bitched about the Eagles.

"Good news," said Liza, four months later. Karla was by the pool with Honey. They were trying to think of other bands with food names.

"Meat Loaf," Honey offered.

"An exciting prospect," Liza said, long-distance. "A last-minute option."

"We're going to Kuwait?" Karla said into the cell phone. "Baghdad?"

Honey giggled. They'd each had an afternoon screwdriver. "Bread," Honey whispered. "Hot Tuna."

"Wrong," said Liza. "Shanghai."

"Shanghai," Karla repeated, testing it out.

"That's not a food," said Ray (Milk), who was wading with Jack in the shallow end. He balanced his can of Guinness on the pool ledge.

"There's just one thing," said Liza. She expelled a long, mentholated cough. "The visas. Very difficult to secure. A perfectly safe city, you understand—but it's a little tricky. And so the contract is a bit longer than usual."

"Six months?"

"Eight, actually. Which will be a great relief, come six months! Almost three times as long as usual—quite an opportunity."

Eight months of commission for Liza. Less money spent by the hotel on equipment schlepping and plane tickets.

"That's a while," said Karla.

"But China—quite a coup."

And Jack would think so, too, she knew. Eight months. It wasn't that long, was it?

"Lucky bitch," said Honey, when Karla hung up.

"Ching Chong!" said Ray, and disappeared under the artificial waterfall.

"Meat Loaf is one guy, not a band," Jack said, wrapping a towel around his expanding waist. To Karla he said, "We should do it."

Karla bought the updated Lonely Planet but told no one at home—she didn't want to jinx it. In her sun lounger she dozed and pictured those sleek, sexy dresses with the high collars. She would have one made, in red silk with tiny white flowers, with a perfect matching purse.

But after Liza's call, as Karla swam her laps and shaved her legs and rattled her tambourine, her worries crept in. Time had begun both to expand and contract in frightening ways. The individual six-night weeks sometimes seemed endless, but the contracts passed quickly: three months times five made fifteen months, a year and a quarter. A great chunk of time was suddenly gone, eaten up, by this odd experiment. She was tired of talking to Honey and working hard on her tan. She was tired of fighting with Jack about song choices or drink choices or the unhealthy hours they kept. She was sick of propping up his lyrics folder nightly.

In Shanghai they could start over: a new continent, a discerning clientele. *Shanghai.* It meant "By the Sea," Karla read. Stunningly chic women. Something about Noël Coward and a long, famous strip along the water with distinctive buildings. It would be cosmopolitan. Karla would be able to sing jazz standards, and no one would have heard of Cher. She would be beautiful in her new silky dress, and Jack would think so, too.

✧

KARLA'S FRIENDS at home—Boston friends and Maine friends—had been interested at first. During the first duo year they'd e-mailed regularly, and when Karla replied she lied a little; she told them she had twelve sets of matching shoes and handbags. She said every night was prom night.

In fact, Karla wore slips that needed to be washed and heels that, although a little too low for her height, caused an ache in her lower back an hour into each night. She wore rhinestone barrettes with missing stones. Her long dresses were in need of rehemming—one dipped a bit too far on one side. One dress was a little too loose around the bust. Another was too tight, flattening her breasts to an extreme. They sickened her lately, these heavy, worn clothes in pinks and blacks and reds. But on her body the dresses felt airy, transparent. People could see right through, she worried. She memorized every mirror in each new hotel: the full-length one by the elevator, the three-quarter-length in the lobby, the one behind the bar where she could see herself from stage, right beside Jack. She looked, she hoped, like she was singing to some distant muse when really she was checking herself out, making sure she wasn't slouching or snapping too frenetically or gripping the microphone stand in an obvious way. Guests blocked her reflection and she willed them to move one inch to the left—*just an inch!*—so she could see herself clearly again.

Jack looked the same each night, in a bright shirt, ironed by her, and black pants and shiny shoes he polished nightly with a compact Kmart shoe sponge, a stocking stuffer Karla had purchased during her last break at home. This had tickled Jack, the idea of Kmart, and this thing called a Blue Light Special, which some comedian had made a joke about at a holiday camp when he was a boy. Karla tried to tell him that it didn't really exist anymore and that she'd never been entirely sure what it was to begin with, but he insisted on using it in conversation from time to time, usually at dinner. "I'll have the Blue Light Special." He had less patience for geography, and for the American pronunciations of certain place names. (Arkansas should be Ar-KANsas, he reasoned.) For a long while, he thought Maine and Massachusetts were one state. He'd never been interested in the vastly different pop charts, or in the way she chose to caffeinate herself.

Jack had told her about his north, about miners and mining disease and his grandfather, who'd worked down there for decades. His grandfather liked to say, "Never trust a man who doesn't drink," and now Jack said this to Karla whenever they were out and she ordered a ginger ale, which wasn't often. She was supposed to laugh when he said this, but she didn't, and then they inevitably had a discussion about the American bar scene versus British pubs and how trendy it was a few years ago for Brits to drink Bud and how the Bud in Europe tasted much better, and how most microbrews were shite.

This he knew: pubs, miners, soccer, the lyrics to every song from *The Commitments,* and now, thanks to her, most of the Carole King songbook. He knew jokes, and he tried them out on her, not just for practice but to make her laugh.

Guests sometimes said that Karla and Jack had no accents when they sang, but they were wrong. There were certain lyrics, certain *aah*s, especially, that were distinctly hers or his. For a year now Karla had wanted to say, "You know in 'Lady in Red,' when you say 'dahncing'? Couldn't you just say 'dancing'?" But this would make her sound like an asshole. She became the one who blended, as she'd been taught to do in her college *a cappella* group. She made herself sound like a proper Geordie, like Sting had once sounded, to fit in.

Karla packed up her dresses and shoes in Muscat before their nonstop flight to London, where they would apply for visas at the Chinese Embassy. Under the heels of her least-favorite pumps, she found a page of notes from Abu Dhabi, contract one, on creased hotel stationery. The pen had dried up on the last few words, and the tip had poked through the paper. She could see exactly where her frustrated hand had dug in, trying to make the ink flow.

She had written:

The cold water is hot enough to shower in. The cold is actually too *hot, sometimes. (The only real cold water I've found is the bottled kind, in the minibar.) In the shower I have to lather quickly, sweating, and get out into the air-conditioned room as soon as possible.*

That was all. She read it twice and threw it away.

THREE

Sade

IN SHANGHAI, no one seemed to care that Karla and Jack had different accents. English was English, and ballads were preferable to anything remotely up-tempo. The Shanghainese were tremendously saddened by the death of Princess Diana, and "Candle in the Wind," the new version, continued to be the most popular request. The Shanghai Airport gift shops sold tea towels with Princess Diana's face framed in a royal oval, next to a prim, unsmiling Prince Charles.

In Shanghai, Karla began to drink white wine in earnest. This was in keeping with the beige motif of the hotel, she reasoned. She knew, thanks to Zahid, that cold things would make her delicate vocal cords turn hard and resistant, like taffy, but she drank her whites chilled anyway, feeling rebellious. Red wine has a tendency to produce mucus, and this would make Karla have to clear her throat onstage, a little involuntary grumble booming out through their Sounds 'N

Pounds speakers. And reds would stain her teeth, the berry mucus accumulating, oxidizing, eating away at good, pure enamel. She may as well have been a smoker. Overall, white wine seemed less risky.

She considered these details cyclically as she crossed Zhong Lu, the thoroughfare separating the twenty-five-story Shanghai Palace Hotel from the 24 Hour Buy Store, where Karla could purchase her wine. The sidewalks were street-like, too, with bikes careening between pedestrians. There wasn't enough space between people. Karla was touched by strangers often, jolted from her thoughts by walkers knocking elbows into her. Everyone pushed and shoved, but not angrily—the expressions on their faces were calm; they were used to it—and to Karla this seemed counterintuitive. If she was going to be jolted, she wanted to bump back, scream a little, stamp her foot. She knew this would have shocked the Shanghainese.

But the 24 Hour Buy Store was relatively uncrowded, and it lived up to its name. Karla could come whenever she wanted. Savvy Palace guests could buy beer and milk and tea and chocolate for a tenth of the room-service prices and store what would fit in the minibar. Karla liked the cool fluorescence, the aisles and choices. She stayed as long as she could in a contented state of indecision.

Today Karla chose Imperial Court White because the label featured pink bamboo leaves. She cradled the bottle, and smoothed her fifty yuan on the counter, and waited for the efficient cashier to swath the glass in cheap plastic—*two* bags, please—which would go straight into the tiny hotel garbage pail. The two bags would disguise the shape and the label of the bottle, Karla liked to think.

She wanted to speak to the cashier, so she said, "*Nee how.*" At home, Karla would have added, "Hot today," but she couldn't remember the words for "hot" or "today," or the tones to match. She waited for her plastic bags and managed "*Shay shay.*" The cashier said nothing.

She crossed Zhong Lu, spun through the revolving doors, and nodded to the concierge in his red jacket with gold-brocade trim. Her high-heeled boots clicked pleasingly against the marble lobby floor—white marble, arched ceiling, elaborately potted flower arrangements providing touches of yellow and orange. There were a few guests in the lobby, and she scanned these faces quickly—none she recognized. She only had to make it to the elevator, where a tall, militant bellboy spoke to her: "Good afternoon, Ka-la." He slapped at the up button before she could.

If someone else had been inside the elevator, and if that someone had made an attempt at friendly chatter, Karla would have been forced out of herself that afternoon. She would have smiled and nodded, said, at floor 18, "Well, this is me." She would have remembered Ava the Cruise Director's catchphrase, "It costs nothing to smile." The imaginary elevator person might see Karla and Jack's photograph in the lobby and come up to the Sky Bar for a drink, and if Karla had been friendly enough, sparkly enough, the guest would clap, and perhaps buy them drinks, and perhaps even tip them. (A Japanese guest had left them ten thousand yen last week for playing "Close to You.") And Jack would be happy and the bar staff would be happy and the Palace General Manager would hear about it and Liza would hear about it and they'd be sent somewhere like Bermuda next time, all because of Karla's smile in the elevator.

Karla got out at 18, swiped her room key, and let the door slip open and click heavily shut behind her. The room smelled like lemon, and the bed was tucked in in all the right places. She stowed the Imperial Court in the tiny fridge. She sat on the couch. She peeled off her tube socks and examined the elastic marks on her calves.

THERE WERE chocolates in the room when they first arrived, on a big white plate with "Welcome to Shanghai" drizzled in perfect bittersweet cursive. There was a fruit basket with ripe bananas and apples and oranges, which they ate immediately, feeling empty and gassy from the airplane food.

There were the standard toiletries—impossibly small bottles of lotion and bath foam, which disappeared, sadly, after three days, as did the contents of the minibar and the lovely, plush, white bathrobes. The slippers stayed but were never worn. They were one size fits all and didn't.

Everything was beige: the carpet, the sheets, the curtains, the frame of the large, circular mirror above the desk, which reminded Karla of *Charlie's Angels*. There was a modest couch, upholstered in silky brown and white stripes. (A love seat, Jack informed her.) They hadn't had a couch before, and it seemed like good luck, something they could use together, or not. They could fight without saying, "I'm sleeping in the bathtub," which Karla had said once, in Doha. And now Karla could take naps on the couch with a beige pillow and beige blanket, facing the window, looking out on a crowded corner of Zhong Lu. This was not the same as going back to bed. This was going back to couch.

Karla was considering a couch nap, or an early glass of Imperial White, when the door swooshed open and Jack appeared, ruddy from squash. He dropped his gym bag on the carpet and nodded, which meant "What are you up to, love?"

She nodded back, meaning "Very fucking little."

"Who's in a bad mood, then?" he said. His T-shirt was bright blue, his collar stained with sweat.

Had she said it out loud?

She heard him splash water on his face and blow his nose, and she knew next he would rummage in the duffel bag for his lighter and spark a well-deserved cigarette.

Not in here—don't even think about it.

He winked and opened the door and blew his smoke into the hallway.

✧

THE SKY BAR was on the twenty-fifth floor of the Palace Hotel, with glass walls on three sides. The city by day was smoggy and complicated, with a jagged skyline, the more modern hotels putting the dated Palace somewhat to shame. The Palace had been the first and the tallest in 1973. The second-tier buildings, which the Palace now resembled, were blocky and functional.

The bar, in daylight, was in need of reupholstering. The carpets had tread marks, and the leather barstools were worn. But at night the room was transformed by small, white tea candles and fresh, voluptuous bouquets. The light was so dim the guests appeared to be floating from Karla's stage view. The light was the same inside and out. The candle points jerked sweetly and the cityscape twinkled, the puzzle of building edges now gone. The pretty waitresses glided by in sleek, black *qi pao*s, and the tasteful duo played tasteful English music. At the Sky Bar, guests could perch high above Shanghai and sit close at tiny tables. They could drink from sexy wineglasses and look just like the city outside: smoothed over, airbrushed by the absence of light.

But often, the duo didn't play tasteful music. They ignored requests for the Carpenters and John Denver. The guitarist liked rock and roll—Elvis, or worse—and the singer kept rattling her tambourine. She sometimes looked sad, and her dresses didn't always fit right. They took long breaks and sat right down at the tables with guests who spoke English, talking loudly and drinking a glass of wine each in twenty minutes flat.

THE FIRST TO introduce herself was the Sky Bar hostess. She was very tall. Karla had to lift her chin to speak to her.

"I am Willow," said the girl.

Karla tried to think of the right response.

"I am Willow, like the tree," she said, and let her arms hang loose like drooping branches.

Jack would make fun of this later, but at the time it seemed lovely.

"What's your real name?" Karla asked.

"You mean Chinese name?" She spoke carefully, placing the English words one in front of the other.

"Yes, Chinese name."

"Hao...Chi...Dian."

"How...Chee...Dee-un," Karla repeated.

"No! Hao Chi *Di*an."

"How Chee *Dee*-un."

"Yes! But you can call me Willow."

THEY MET SAM the Bar Manager, who told them his dog had died.

"That's terrible," Karla said.

"And also she was blind." Sam looked past her, at the wall of windows. His head was a perfect circle.

"We're all blind," Karla said. She was on her second glass of chardonnay.

Sam nodded.

✧

MARGARET, THE Head Bartender, asked if they liked salsa dancing—she was going to a class next week.

"*Par-ty. Merengue. Fiesta. Forever,*" she sang.

"All night long," said Jack.

"Maybe," said Karla. "That could be fun."

THEY MET ROLLY, the F and B Manager, hawkeyed and large. He was Greek and he disapproved of Karla's outfits. He called Jack into his office and told him to tell Karla to wear shorter skirts.

"She won't," said Jack.

"She has legs, I presume. She will wear clothing suitable for our clientele."

"You should probably tell her yourself," said Jack.

"I have said it to you. You are her colleague. You can pass on the message, yes?"

But Jack didn't. (She'd find out the truth much, much later. She always found out.) Jack had made the mistake of suggesting something similar in Dubai, and Karla had ignored him for the rest of the day.

"What was that all about?" Karla asked, back in the room.

"Bar sales are up. He wanted to thank us, for bringing in the boozers and entertaining them so well."

"And he couldn't tell me, too?"

"Boy talk. Numbers and sales. He's not enlightened, our Rolly."

"Is it part of the job description or something? To be a sexist ass if you're an F and B guy?"

"It seems to help," said Jack. *Lighten up,* he meant.

WEEK FOUR WAS dwindling past, one full month in China. They'd met no one beyond the bar, learned no new music. "I'm bored," Karla said, from the couch. She didn't bother explaining.

"Well, don't be," Jack said carefully. He had no idea what she meant.

"We need to learn songs, new ones," she said.

"Be my guest," he said, and reached for his racquet.

FOUR

Captain & Tennille

By the time they got to Shanghai, Karla and Jack knew over four hundred songs. Fifty-three were acoustic numbers, just guitar and two voices, and these were Northern Lights' strongest numbers—Ralph McTell, Don McLean, Carole King, Simon and Garfunkel, random Crowded House songs Jack had covered in his school band, and Joni Mitchell, of course. This was where they merged most convincingly: Joni Mitchell. Jack and Karla knew, just as Ava the Cruise Director had known, that they were legitimate in this sense. Karla had the earnest look of the protest singer. Jack provided the laughs.

But you couldn't dance to folksy. You couldn't do four hours of "Both Sides Now."

Their Shanghai contract stipulated they learn new songs each week. This was standard for Asia, Liza explained, and rarely enforced. But Karla began to make a list of requests they received and didn't know and new songs she'd heard and liked and new songs she didn't like and knew would soon be requested. She tried to order some of each, a variety of tracks.

Not songs, but *tracks,* because the music was prerecorded on minidisc, minus the vocals and the guitar. They could opt, when ordering their tracks, to erase certain parts, and those missing parts were what Jack and Karla filled in. This was not something Karla was proud of, necessarily, and it wasn't something her muso friends from school were aware of, although they probably wondered, privately. ("'Love Shack' with just guitar and vocals?") Karla was beginning to feel that she should write a mass e-mail, that she should come clean.

At first, she'd been appropriately offended by the tracks. She'd watched Wight Nights perform in the Tally-Ho Lounge, and, when an Irish woman in a sarong requested "Careless Whisper," she'd been shocked to hear the sax solo without the accompanying saxophone. But Sarong seemed not to notice or care; in fact, she ordered a round of mai tais, the Cocktail of the Day, and had them sent to the stage.

After a week onboard, after seeing Wight Nights daily, Karla was more intrigued than insulted. An orchestral version of Patsy Cline's "Crazy" came on, and Karla thought, before she could catch herself, *Oh, I like this one.* The duo had a black and silver banner draped behind them, their name sparkling, and Karla thought, *Of course.* It wasn't wholly admirable, but it was economical. It was a way to be a band and not be a band. It was a way to work and sing with two.

Now, when Karla placed her orders, she had to choose the appropriate keys. She listened to the original song versions first. She'd sometimes bought the tapes (bootleg versions with Arabic liner notes from Dubai Song Galleria or, now, with Chinese liner notes from Big Yankee Music), but, often, she simply waited to hear the songs on English radio stations, as she'd done back in York. This method was tricky. She sang along, and if the song was too high or too low, she had to adjust it accordingly. She kept the starting note in her head and ran to find her pitch pipe and tried to match the note with one of twelve. She hoped it was right. (Could she have shifted down or up a half step, while scurrying for the pipe?) It was probably right. She wrote it down. ("Under the Boardwalk"—starts on A?) She used the cocktail piano in the lobby lounge either early in the morning or very late at night, and she picked out the first verse, slowly. She took it down a half step. (She'd taken just enough music theory to do this.) She sang the transposed version, all the way through, and felt it was still too high. She took it down another step. But if she took it down too far, it became a different song.

Jack had pointed this out. "It doesn't sound right anymore," he'd said of her transposed "Without You," the Mariah Carey version.

"It doesn't sound right with me screeching after the key change," she replied.

Karla transposed for Jack, too. He could have done this himself on his guitar, but he didn't. She played the original when he happened to be in the room and asked if the key was okay. But it was hard to make him sing the song all the way through, past the bridge or the modulation, and so she had to guess sometimes. If she guessed wrong, the tracks were wasted.

She could be annoying about this, she knew. She tried not to be. She guessed and hoped for the best.

Another option was to buy "Rock Out With..." CDs from music stores. So far they had rocked out with Led Zeppelin, the Clash, and Alanis Morissette, and Karla had her eye on Blondie. She was pleased with herself for discovering this option: eight tracks, sans guitar, for twenty-five dollars. But the Rock Out people were clever. They never put too many hits on one CD—one or two, maybe three, and the remaining five were obscure B-sides. And the keys couldn't be adjusted.

When they started out, Jack and Karla had 150 tracks in their possession, all donated by Wight Nights. Because Zak played bass and Macy played keyboards, the tracks were guitar-heavy, with quiet drums. Jack said Karla should play tambourine, for added rhythm, and it would sound fine.

It didn't sound fine, but they used them anyway.

The tracks Karla chose now were expensive, ten dollars each, but they were recorded with real instruments, not the quack-quack keyboards of the cheaper versions. Karla waited for specials—ten songs for $70, or twenty for $125, and when the packages arrived from California (Magic Trax) or Middlesex (Songsmiths), she typed up the words and put them in their lyrics folders. As established in York, the theory was to have one *thin* folder of new lyrics each, to use onstage only when necessary. Once memorized, the lyrics sheet would be pulled.

Karla had since given up on Jack's lyrics folder, but she continued to memorize her own. She tested herself as she walked to and from the post office or during her laps in the pool. She went to their bar before opening time and practiced new songs on the microphone. Her voice, amplified: It still confused and thrilled her, after all these nights.

JACK WAS THE official mike speaker, although this hadn't always been the case. In Abu Dhabi and Dubai, Karla had babbled and giggled and said whatever came to mind. But in Doha they'd had a terrible fight and Jack had said he couldn't stand it anymore. He'd wanted to say it for months, and so he did: She should not be allowed to speak on the mike, *ever.*

At the time Karla had said all the right things. (Fuck off, she'd speak when she fucking wanted to and what fucking Dark Age did he think he was fucking living in?) But it stuck, and afterward she said little. She introduced songs matter-of-factly when he couldn't remember the artist or title. She said thank you three or four times after each song, just to let the guests know she *could* speak. She sometimes laughed at his jokes.

She told herself this wasn't wimpy behavior on her part but coworker adjustment. He preferred she say less. He had told her so. She preferred he sing verses in the right order, and keep to his designated melody. These were the negotiations they made, sharing the same workspace.

This left Karla in charge of two things onstage:

1. Making sure music came on the moment their set was through. (The importance of play-off music had been emphasized on the ship—never allow for a moment of awkward silence.)
2. Suggesting, as quickly as possible, the song they should play next.

It was tricky. They couldn't predict what a given audience would want to hear on a given night. They did know that if a song was well received, they should roll with it and play similar songs in sequence. For that reason "Take Me Home, Country Roads" and "Nine to Five" were on the same prerecorded minidisc, and "Ain't No Sunshine" and "I Heard It Through the Grapevine" were on another. They had a Ballad Disc and an ABBA Disc. They had something called Random Disc, which was all the songs they liked to play and no one knew (Indigo Girls, Sex Pistols).

Inevitably, requests came in for songs on very different discs. Karla had a list on her music stand, organized alphabetically by song title, and she used this to find the disc number and track number while Jack made up things to say. The list was printed in a very small font. (There were so many songs, and it would look bad to have too many pages to flip through.) And so Karla squinted, and tried not to panic, and prayed for the awkward pauses to pass quickly.

When they left each night, they took their microphones and their discs. The rest they covered with black tablecloths. In Dubai, Jack's effects pedal had been stolen. In Doha, someone had cut their wires. It was very neatly done, with scissors. Jack had been thrilled—a night off! But to Karla it was creepy. Wouldn't someone get his hand chopped off for this? Who would have done it? A drunk local? An angry cleaner?

"Someone who hates the Eagles," Jack said.

BEFORE THE FIRST contract, Jack and Karla had spent an entire day in Newcastle in a music store called Sounds 'N Pounds, where Karla had felt very much like a dumb girl. Jack made her try out the microphones in the store. She sang "Black Velvet," and no one seemed to notice.

They left with a mixing desk, speakers, amplifiers, a spare electric guitar, mike stands, speaker stands, music stands, a minidisc player-recorder, a CD player, leads, a large effects pedal for Jack, and one jangly tambourine for Karla. (She'd had her eye on an egg shaker, too, but that could wait.) Jack put it all on his credit card.

It was now understood that Karla owned the minidisc tracks and Jack owned the rest. If they should ever split, Karla would need the backup and Jack, theoretically, would not. It was fair, Jack explained.

It was fair, but it was irritating. In the store, Karla had calculated how much she owed and how much she could afford to pay each month, and on the way back to York she'd made her offer. But Jack said no, he didn't want her to contribute. It was his Geordie chivalry emerging, she thought. His father had probably told him this was the right thing to do.

And so she let him pay; she assumed they'd be investing in new equipment someday, together. She'd chip in then. But the only new equipment they acquired was the egg shaker Karla finally splurged on, in a toy store in the Dubai Citi-Center Mall. It was shaped like a strawberry instead of an egg.

KARLA DECIDED to include a brief note with her next Magic Trax order form. "Hey, Mike! Hope you're doing well in Cally. We're in Shanghai and hope to escape soon. I'm psyched about the new All Saints track. Bye, Karla."

To which Mike responded: "We have a database of Acts we send trax to and if you'd like to be on file, we'd luv 2 have a picture from you guys. My boss asked me to ask you." *Lie,* Karla knew, but she enclosed their glossy anyway, the same eight-by-ten from the ship they'd been using since Abu Dhabi. She looked at it carefully for the first time in months. They were in their evening wear, bright-eyed and tan. Karla wore her favorite red dress, and her hair was curly from humidity. They were little starlets, out at sea. There was so much for them to do and see together, and they would *do* it, with their bright, bright teeth and smiles.

They didn't look like that anymore. And when you didn't look like your photo, it was time to quit or change your photo.

FIVE

Wham!

JACK AND KARLA TRIED hard to abide by the one-inch curtain gap rule. They deliberately left a crack before bed, a space where daylight could slice through. It was Jack's idea, and Karla approved. They knew a lack of light could ruin things, make them sleep too long—snaked, sweating—waking with thick heads to yell at each other over nothing, guilty from the afternoon.

Except on Sunday, their day off. On Saturday night, they left no crack.

On their fifth Sunday in Shanghai, Karla woke early anyway, startled by a sound outside their room, a plastic bag swishing and the tap of a wire hanger placed on their metal doorknob. Their dry cleaning, delivered: 9:30 A.M. They still had time. Karla tried to sleep again, but the body beside her was farting a little and taking up too much room. She clutched at him. It was the only thing to do. She wrapped herself around the solid mass of him, linking a leg around his.

When at last Karla forced herself up, she checked her

watch (Gold Market, Dubai) and cringed: 11:34. "We suck," she said, and roused Jack. She kept the curtain closed—she wanted to ease into this day carefully, without irritating herself further.

Karla craved waffles with strawberries and cream, but it would be too busy in the Continental Café to have brunch. They were allowed to eat in four of the eight Palace restaurants but never during peak times. Instead they took the elevator straight down to the basement-level Fast Snack, a Chinese diner with rows of aquariums along one wall, the meal options swimming or crawling right there at the entrance. Karla ordered vegetable buns and red bean paste squares without looking at the menu. Jack asked for the sweet and sour pork.

"Boat ride," said Jack, looking up from the *China Daily*, which he'd propped against the soy sauce bottle. They could take a cruise along the Huangpu River. He tapped the ad on the newspaper page with his fork and left a smudge of orange sauce.

Yes, a boat ride, like being back on the ship. Water and motion and Jack's jokes about lifeboat drills. This would be a good thing.

They ate quickly and signed the guest check and elevated back upstairs to retrieve their things (camera, sunglasses, guidebook, money, bottle of water). They descended and pushed their way around the revolving doors—into cold and drizzle. They hadn't thought of this; the curtain had been closed, the basement cheerfully fluorescent. And now everywhere there were bicycles and figures in ponchos.

It was beautiful, like hundreds of E.T.'s spinning by in plastic primary colors, about to rise and glide away.

"The colors," Karla said.

"Shit," said Jack, looking up at the sky, which was a sickly gray-white.

"We could do something else," she said. "The temple. Jing'An Temple. It's yellow." Just a short walk, and they wouldn't get that wet.

"It's yellow?" Jack said.

"They're all yellow—"

"I know, I read that, too," he said, and lit a cigarette. "I mean, does the color matter?"

"It's kind of cool."

Jack kept his distance from religious landmarks. He'd explained in Abu Dhabi, when she'd wanted to see a mosque. He thought it was disrespectful to be a tourist in that way, to step inside without believing. But all the bicycles and colors in the rain—it *felt* religious, and Karla wanted to keep looking. She wanted a walk in the rain with her boyfriend, to the temple or wherever.

"Bad day," Jack said, and then, seeing her face, added, "Sorry." He squashed his cigarette stub with his heel. He was going back upstairs to do some laptop work. It was a good day for that. "Coming in?"

Where else could she go? The 24 Hour Buy Store? A bottle of white was already chilling in the minibar. She could invent errands to run on Nanjing Lu, as she had last Sunday. She could stay right there and watch the bicycles without him, but the doorman would begin to fidget and wonder.

"I guess," she said, and together they went back in.

Karla claimed the couch and began to read *Lolita* with Chinese footnotes, which she'd found in the Shanghai Foreign Language Bookstore, for ten yuan. Once it was dark, she would be allowed to have her first glass of wine.

She would read exactly half of *Lolita* today, she decided, and thought of Mom in the window seat after work, in her wool socks and slippers. Mom might be reading now, a thick, hardback murder mystery in crackling library cellophane. No, it was the wrong time of day. She'd be sleeping.

"You're a little bookworm, aren't you?" Jack said, looking up from his laptop, placing an empty bottle of Tsingtao in the tiny beige pail. It was large enough for exactly three bottles.

Bookworm? He seemed surprised, as though he was just realizing this about her.

"I like books," said Karla, without looking up. She pretended to be rapt, absorbed, but he'd ruined it. She was self-conscious now, a *reader.*

"It's getting dark," Karla announced.

"It will be soon," said Jack. He was typing quickly, pausing only to take sips.

She opened the minibar.

✧

THE NEXT SUNDAY they were prepared, not for the boat ride but for the Shanghai Acrobatic Show. Karla had purchased tickets in advance. She'd finished *Lolita* that afternoon, and it would be good to be out after another long day with Humbert Humbert.

The concierge translated the address into kanji, and the cabbie dropped them off just in time. The theater was damp and poorly lit. They watched from the third row as unsmiling, leotarded Chinese boys bounded through rings the size of hula hoops and twirled plates on top of very tall rods. There were sweat marks under their armpits.

"That was interesting," said Karla, once she was bundled in her puffy winter coat.

"They like their plates," said Jack. They crossed Nanjing Lu, and he gripped her hand until they reached the sidewalk, just as her father used to do in heavy traffic. Lights blinked around them, neon storefronts and stalls. A boy swept at a green puddle with a straw broom. A brown loafer floated near the curb.

They stopped at a stationery store, where Karla bought a red photo album that folded back and forth like an accordion. "Very Chinese," Jack said. It was for wedding pictures—Karla wasn't sure how she knew this. The cashier counted change on an abacus, bored, flipping the wooden beads quickly.

They reached the Bund, where the Pudong Oriental Pearl Tower flashed from across the river. Such an odd, alien beacon—green vertical beams and red balls interspersed, glittering like Christmas in space. "The Pudong presence," Karla said. "We must obey."

They decided to try the bar in the Peace Hotel, "the most famous hotel in the world"—dark wood, small tables. The waitress gave them a drink menu and a song menu for the Peace Jazz Band. The Chinese bandleader, on trumpet, smiled into the air, wise and serene. Two tall tourists in windbreakers (Scandinavian?) danced awkwardly. Jack and Karla watched them without speaking and ordered another round.

"Want a song? Or a dance?" Jack read the options aloud: "'Slow Boat to China,' 'When the Saints Go Marching In,' 'I Left My Heart in San Francisco'—"

"No thanks," Karla said.

She would regret this. She should have danced with Jack in the most famous hotel in the world.

"We play them," she added. "It seems weird to make a request."

She knew what was coming: a joke, a diversion. "Be honest," he said. "You want 'Candle in the Wind.'"

Not one of his better ones, but she was grateful. "Yup," she said, and clinked her glass with his.

✧

THE LAPTOP WORK Jack did was business-related. He was building something daily, something called JOE, which stood for Jack's Overseas Entertainment. (He liked the Overseas part, which Karla had suggested.) He had business cards made up, the *J* shaped like a quarter note, "International Booking Agency" in bold, raised print.

"If Liza can make money from us, then I can make money from other poor tossers."

"She'll find out," Karla said.

"Free market," said Jack.

Not in China.

Jack advertised in *The Stage* back home for "self-contained girl-boy duos" and promised "exclusive engagements in Asian and Middle Eastern five-star hotels. All found."

"All found?" Karla asked.

"All found. Everything included. Flights, accommodation, meals."

"You made that up."

"I didn't. It's the lingo, Karla. It's what we do—you've heard it before."

"I haven't. Not ever."

It was enticing: *all found.* If she'd heard it, she would've felt slightly better about their job.

Jack's school friend picked up the weekly JOE submissions from a P.O. box in York and forwarded them in padded envelopes. They were hand-delivered to their room by a fresh-faced bellboy, a stamp collector who liked the royal profiles in muted colors: forest green, burnt sienna. He had a collection, and he asked Karla to peel them off carefully. Jack recycled the padded envelopes. Nothing was wasted.

The video submissions were poorly recorded in small, empty bars like the one Karla and Jack had first played in Abu Dhabi. The girls wore leather skirts and high boots and squeezed themselves into halter tops. The guys played keyboards or guitar and were twenty years older. They had pronounced facial hair or leather pants or both.

Karla felt better, watching the tapes. Her wardrobe seemed classy. She didn't own any leather. Her legs looked much better than theirs in short skirts. Jack wasn't *that* much older.

She was beginning to understand how they appeared to F and B Managers: modest, wholesome. Jack was clean-shaven and Karla didn't emphasize cleavage, and not just because it wasn't an option. In Dubai, the Bangladeshi Bar Manager had once asked, smiling, if she was a Muslim; she never showed her skin.

JACK BEGAN TO devote four hours each day to JOE because four hours of JOE plus four Sky Bar hours equaled eight total hours of work. Eight hours was normal, respectable.

For a while, he got up at 9:30. (Karla focused a lazy eye on the clock to check.) By 10:00, he said, he was seated in the Business Center, his laptop plugged in and whirring. It was more like a real job that way, beyond the room. He permitted himself one cigarette break per hour and thirty minutes for lunch at Fast Snack. By 2:30 he was done.

By 3:15 he was on the squash court. At 5:30 P.M. he steam-bathed and Jacuzzied, then showered and shaved. At 7:00 P.M. the room would be empty. (Karla ordered wine before dinner and liked to savor it.) He slipped in to choose a dry-cleaned pair of trousers and to have his first bottle of Tsingtao, bought by Karla and chilled all afternoon. At 7:30 P.M. he joined Karla in the dining room, where she would be waiting in a dress that matched his shirt. This was briefly discussed before he left each morning, or left in a note. ("J—Wear blue. K.")

"Impressive," said Karla, the first night he strolled in to dinner from the gym. Her hair was damp, and this bothered him, she knew. *Unprofessional.* She caught her reflection in the wall mirror beyond the buffet table and tried not to watch herself.

Jack had said she looked smaller in China.

"What, shorter?" she'd said. She was taller than all the girls but Willow.

But she knew what he meant. On the ship she'd consumed more—ice cream, piña coladas. She'd laughed more. She was shrinking now, becoming tighter, less buoyant.

Karla brought her book to dinner the next night and the next, and when Jack came in from the gym, she pretended not to see him until he pushed the empty chair away from the table, abruptly. He wanted her to laugh at herself for being so absorbed, get *out* of herself for a moment. She could see all this, but it didn't make her act the way he wanted her to. And because she didn't smile or laugh or look surprised, he was at a loss, nightly. He spoke immediately to fill the gap.

"Raining like a bastard today."

She nodded.

He complained about a letter he'd spent an hour composing and then forgotten to save, and about the grouchy secretary in the Business Center who still made him pay for printed pages.

Karla glanced at her open book.

He told her about the Bar Blue contract, in Abu Dhabi. They needed a duo to start in one month, and if Jack could find someone in time, he'd get it. Ten percent of the duo's salary, which was exactly what Jack and Karla still paid Liza every month. With ten duos, this would be worth something. With twenty it would be even better. A band earned more, so he'd make more with a five- or six-piece, but duos were a start.

She knew all this, but he kept going.

"Liza got it instead," he reported. "I just found out."

"Hm?"

"The Bar Blue contract. She got it." Liza again. They needed to break from her, he said, if they ever expected the agency to grow.

He was done. He waited for her to speak.

She said nothing. She sipped her wine and waited for him to ask.

But he didn't ask, not yet. He needed to order—he had exactly an hour before his other job began. He waited for his appetizer and his drink. He smoothed his napkin on his lap until all the wrinkles were gone.

"So what did you do today?" he asked.

Her smile came then, meek but there. *Start with that, why don't you?* Her hair was drying; she could feel it lifting away from her skull.

Jack smiled back and noticed her gold bracelet, the one he'd bought for her in Saint Martin.

"*Dripping* with gold," he said, and they both looked at it, little dolphins linked together by impossibly small stars.

✧

KARLA SUPPORTED JOE, in theory. Jack wanted to build something. He was preparing for the after-duo phase, and she was touched by this. She volunteered to go on errands (twenty large envelopes, fifteen folders, one glue stick). She helped with the mass mailings. She addressed, she licked, she schlepped to the post office, where there was no line but a crowd with hands outstretched. If you held back, as Karla had at first, no one helped you.

Karla whined about the post office, but she was often grateful for the errands. On days when her help wasn't required, she slept in and woke up stiff. The beige lulled her. It made her days fuzzy and disorganized. A good day meant waking up without a headache, leaving the room before noon, and checking her e-mail in the Business Center, where Jack would mumble a few words about Liza or remind her to pick up beer. A better day meant all this plus going to the gym, memorizing a new song, and finding chocolate cake at the evening buffet.

Karla decided she wasn't getting the REM sleep she needed. She'd done a science project on dreams in seventh grade, and she remembered the REM cycles come in fours. She and Jack worked 9:00 P.M. to 1:00 A.M. They started when most people were winding down, and were winding down when most people were enjoying their first cycle of REM.

At a certain point (At what point was it, exactly? Where had they been?) the duo thing had become not an experiment but their lives. Karla had begun to have cravings for grilled cheese sandwiches and bowls of Cheerios at 2:00 A.M. She wanted shelves and CD racks. She missed her parents.

She remembered marking a page in an IKEA catalog her mother had sent, upon request, all the way to Doha—the page featured whites and blues, bare wooden floors, a corner desk for list making. It was the perfect room. Where was the page, the catalog? In her suitcase? Thrown out by Housekeeping?

The mandatory shaft of light through the curtains was a killer lately, reminding her: *Perfect day. Your guidebook is gathering dust.* The binding was still pristine, unbent. It was late March and she still hadn't seen the museum or the Yu Yuan Garden. She hadn't eaten dim sum in the Old City or crossed the bridge to Pudong.

THE NEXT AFTERNOON Karla opened the blinds and watched the traffic on Zhong Lu. No rain. She dressed quickly without showering and left the required note for Jack. She asked the concierge to translate "People's Square," but he wrote "People's Park" instead. On purpose? It didn't matter, she supposed—people were people. She tipped the taxi driver excessively and slammed the door behind her without meaning to.

So this was China.

The park was made of stone—stone benches, pebbled paths, symmetrical boulders placed at equidistant intervals—and anemic trees with mottled bark. There was an admission charge, but Karla wandered in, playing the foreigner card. She was in the mood to get caught, and she was, by a hunched, uniformed woman who marched over and firmly requested one yuan. The woman had deep pockets in faded tan pants and few teeth. She snatched Karla's coin and turned away.

There were couples everywhere, smooching on top of boulders and under trees, on necks and lips and cheeks and hands. Some of these kisses were long and involved, and it was hard for Karla not to stare, hands slowly creeping up shirts and down pants. *These couples want to be fucking,* she thought. Old men played checkers, and old women practiced tai chi under the splotchy trees. Mothers held babies, and fathers stood apart, walking with their hands behind their backs, as if solving complicated equations in their heads.

There was no rush in People's Park. Karla needed rush or, at the very least, a hand down her pants, an equation to solve. A ship in her goddamned harbor.

Karla paid one yuan for toilet paper but couldn't go. There was one long gutter in the floor and a lady crouched over it, squatting just so. Karla saved her paper for later.

People's Square had actual grass, she'd heard, and she knew it wasn't too far away. She liked maps (more than guidebooks), and she'd studied them back in the room when Jack was gone sometimes, vaguely preparing for days outside. She'd yet to find the right pocket map.

On the street, a man with a gray fedora approached and held a note in her face: "Derek Cox, the great American pin-up star." Karla put her hand on her purse, but this wasn't his motive. Had she heard of Derek Cox? She hadn't. The man shrugged and pushed on, in search of the next Caucasian.

The man had lost someone, an actual person.

"The Internet," Jack would say. "The Internet is changing all that. He should go online and find this Cox fellow that way."

She liked her version better. She liked that the man was earnestly looking, the hardest way imaginable.

She found People's Square and the Shanghai Museum entrance, with an unusually green stretch of lawn and a fountain and the underground mall entrance she'd read about. (She'd save the museum for a rainy day.) Everywhere, kids and parents darted around flying kites, trying to build up speed, gripping invisible bits of string, looking up as they ran. But there were no collisions.

Karla aimed her camera at a clear patch of sky, hoping for a pretty assortment of kites. She'd done this once in Margarita, trying to catch pelicans as they dived for fish. (Jack had gone to the bar for two more rum punches.)

And then Karla was done. She'd run out of film and her feet hurt. She would tell Jack about the park and the friend of Derek Cox. Over dinner she would draw it out. She'd do the talking for a change.

✧

KARLA WENT BACK to the Shanghai Foreign Language Bookstore and considered appealing titles:

Fun with Pastry
Cribbage for Dummies
Be an Atari Meister
Living in Sin: Great Hotels in the Great Lakes Region
Crustaceans, a Field Guide
When Alcoholism Finds You
Baked Alaska, a Roadtrip
How to Play with Your Pets
Making Sense of Heavy Metal
E Pluribus What? *Debunking the Melting Pot Myth*

The bookstore was five stories tall and had a pungent smell: mildew and sweat. A boy in baggy shorts read Anaïs Nin in a corner, a maple leaf stitched on his backpack.

"Canadian?" Karla asked.

"Vancouver," he said. He had braces and was too old for braces. He tucked his lips carefully back over his teeth.

"Ever been to Halifax?" Karla asked, remembering Sid the Comedian.

"No. You?"

"No. I'm from Maine."

"Ever been to Hawaii?"

She got it, opposite parts of a vast country. A stupid question. His girlfriend from Winnipeg—she hadn't been to Halifax, either—returned and steered him away.

"I sing at the Palace Sky Bar," Karla called after them.

An Australian lady eyed the alcoholism book Karla still held in her hand. Karla put it back and made her final purchases:

American Psycho
Pride and Prejudice
Beverly Hills 90210: Exposed

The middle one canceled out the other two.

IT RAINED. Karla opened Lonely Planet in bed and read aloud. "'The Shanghai Museum contains ancient coins, bronzes, furniture, gemstones, paintings, porcelain and National Minority crafts.'"

"Riveting," said Jack. He was working on a mass mailing to the Caribbean. He slouched at the desk, still in his boxers.

He couldn't be bothered with the Business Center today—he'd woken up late and there would be no time for squash. He was composing cover letters to every F and B Manager in Saint Lucia. There were 153.

Karla asked if he could include Northern Lights in the Caribbean proposals. He could use a different name on the cover letter, Jackson instead of Jack. She was thinking of long beach days with good books, their tanned, buff bodies swimming close.

But he didn't think it was a good idea. Unprofessional, he said, to lie like that in a cover letter.

She didn't dwell on this. She snapped the guidebook shut. She showered and dressed and wondered how she would describe the modern-looking arcs and angles of the museum facade. *Gaudiesque?* No. She'd liked Intro to Art History, one of her few nonmusic classes. She'd liked the slides and the darkness and memorizing images rather than sounds.

She gathered her purse, said, "I'm going now."

"Have fun, then." His voice was weary, as though he'd just commuted, as though he sat in a cubicle.

"We're in Shanghai," she said, louder than planned. "I want to see Shanghai." *Come with me today,* she meant. *We have a lifetime to compose cover letters.*

"Not stopping you, love." He was waiting for her to go, waiting to open the little fridge and pull out his first Tsingtao.

She gave a little twirl good-bye with her umbrella and went.

✧

BY DINNERTIME Karla had absorbed her irritation and was prepared to give her recap. Her hair was wet from the shower again and her wine was sour from toothpaste. Jack wore bright blue and she wore light blue, to match.

There hadn't been a line, she began, at the museum ticket booth. Just a rush of bodies pushing with calm expressions, like the post-office people.

The crowds, grabbing, made Karla think of her father and his five siblings, all those hungry people at the dinner table, family plus friends, whoever happened to be staying for the night. You snatched your food quickly, her father told her, and you ended up with fork marks on your hands.

In Shanghai, Karla felt like that sometimes—fork-marked.

"Fork-what?"

"You're not listening."

"I am. Can you get the waiter?"

The museum maps were in Chinese, so she'd wandered like the rest of the foreigners into the Jade Room, which was dark and soothing. So many shades of green. Only the display cases were illuminated, and so the tourists were guided by the exhibits, drawn to the lights like bugs. Someone had arranged large potted plants to funnel the flow of traffic. It was so quiet, except for echoes of voices in the marble hallway outside. You had to honor the dark with a hushed kind of reverence. You felt hidden.

He looked up from his grilled salmon.

"It's just nice not to be looked at sometimes, you know? After what we do at night."

"It's the price we pay for fame," said Jack, returning to his plate.

In the Bronze Room, a boy asked to take her picture because she had blond hair. This had happened before—on the Bund, in the malls. She said yes, because other people were watching. Encouraged by the audience, the boy hooked an arm around her waist, which Karla wanted immediately to remove.

"He was just a boy," Jack observed.

"He smelled like Hawaiian Punch."

Then, the Ancient Coins, which were shaped like knives and hatchets, some several inches long, and heavy, by the look of them.

"You would have made a joke about them, I thought, about carrying them around in your pocket or something."

"That would've been funny." He half smiled. She was getting to him, a little.

Even the Gallery of Classical Furniture had been appealing. There were chairs and desks and beds in rich, dark wood, chocolate-colored, polished beyond belief, almost edible-looking, smelling earthy. Exactly the shade of horse manure.

"That's nice."

She pushed on before he had a chance to say more. The Minority Nations Room had faceless mannequins in various forms of traditional dress. There were cases of masks and baskets and chunky jewelry, all reminiscent of Native American things, and lots of photographs of toothless women weaving. Not one of her favorites.

He was waiting for her to finish her chicken salad so he could light his cigarette.

She skipped ahead. "The Seal Room was my favorite." All those little designs in carved soapstone: lions and tigers and birds. Toy treasures, useful and small. These she wanted to touch.

And then she'd decided to see every room. Otherwise she might miss something important.

"How many rooms are left?" asked Jack.

"Not many."

His beer arrived and he took a long sip.

The Chinese Painting Room paintings had simple lines and little color, mostly grays and blacks, and featured lots of mountains and flowers and birds. One was called *Autumn Mountain at Dusk*. Even the titles were tranquil.

"A good name," he agreed. He was getting his buzz on, slowly. How many beers had he had that afternoon?

She'd needed a break then, so she ordered a cup of coffee in the Tea Room for thirty yuan. A waiter delivered a tiny thimble of milk, a plate of sweets (cookies, dried mango, oval-shaped sour things with pits), and a moist cloth to wash her hands. She paid close attention to the white china coffee cup, having visited the Porcelain Room. "Isn't it wild? A kind of pottery named for the country that invented it. *China*. 'Pottery belongs to all mankind, but porcelain is China's invention.'"

"Very nice."

"I'm quoting. From the book."

And then, on her way out, she came across a small room she'd nearly overlooked—

"God forbid."

Renaissance paintings, on loan from the Medici Collections. This room was busier than all the others. Little kids sat on tiny folding stools, sketching with pen and pencil sets. Some were very good. Their mothers were there, watching for perspective and shading.

"*Little* kids. It was amazing."

The big draw had been the Botticelli painting of Mary.

She was long-limbed, arching unnaturally over her baby son. There was a Michelangelo, too, a mold of a small male torso.

"I remember from Florence," he said. "You wanted to see the *David*—the *David*?"

She nodded. He was with her still.

"But we had Port Manning duty that day, right?"

She kept nodding. She wasn't done.

The Michelangelo torso was headless, but still sexy. In fact, after the dull gray mountains and birds, these Renaissance bodies were a great relief. All the paintings featured sculpted pecs with nipples erect and breasts casually revealed through gauze robes. It occurred to her that each figure was a naked body with cloth merely painted onto its hard curves. Even the battle scenes were orgiastic, bodies dead and alive, limbs arching, reaching, twisting—

"Easy," Jack said, looking around.

"They have no idea what I'm saying," she said.

He lit another Marlboro Light and blew away from her.

After that, she said, wrapping up, she'd seen enough. She went to the gift shop and bought the book.

"But I'm going back, to take notes. You should come."

"I feel like I've been there already." His tone was bored but his eyes were jokey, and this made the words funny rather than cruel. The English way.

It had worked—he'd listened, except for the nipples part. And now, four hours of singing together, coworker mode.

"CANDLE IN THE Wind," Jack whispered, an hour later. Willow, smiling brightly, had just placed a request card on his music stand.

"Do we have to?" Karla whispered back. Her strapless bra was inching down, and she wanted nothing more than to tug it back up.

The opening bars of Elton John's invisible piano began to play, and a couple in the back clapped in appreciation.

After work, Karla changed into jeans and a sweatshirt and waited for the elevator to take her to Fast Snack. She would eat dim sum and make herself read *Pride and Prejudice*. Once she finished *Pride and Prejudice*, she would be allowed to begin *90210: Exposed*.

The elevator slid open to reveal a Chinese couple, the "Candle in the Wind" fans. They'd just descended from the Sky Bar, where Jack remained, drinking Manhattans with a tan Texan doctor. The woman clutched a Northern Lights flyer.

Karla smiled and touched her sweatshirt. "I've changed," she said, explaining. The man smiled back, blankly, and the woman giggled. An ugly pause followed as they collectively prayed for the elevator to land and open.

When it did, and the lobby appeared, the couple stepped out. At last the man turned to her, waving the flyer.

"Singer!" he said.

"Yes, I've changed. Done with work."

"Aah. Nice voice."

"Thank you."

The woman nodded.

"Very true," he said.

"Thank you." Her gut jumped with relief. *Nice voice.* "Good night!" Karla said, and down she slid to the basement. She should have said *wan an*.

In Fast Snack, Karla ordered veggie buns, palm-size and warm, with squares of rice paper stuck to the spongy white undersides. She peeled these and pierced each bun with a chopstick and waited. She read five paragraphs. She broke a bun in two and examined the contents—spinach, mostly, with sparse bits of mushroom. Egglike with green nestled safely inside. She loved this—the bun, split and steaming, ready to dip, spongy pieces in soy sauce, warmness spreading in her belly.

She signed her name on the guest check and wrote "Entertainer" underneath.

Jack would be in the room, in his boxers, staring at the TV. She'd tell him about the couple in the elevator, making it funnier than it actually was. He would tease her about having veggie bits in her teeth when she didn't (she'd already checked in the lobby mirror), and he'd tell her what was happening in this episode.

But he wasn't there. It was 2:10 A.M. His wallet was gone, and his blue dress shirt was on the nice wooden hanger, in the closet. There was no note.

IN THE MORNING Karla decided to stroll, unencumbered, through Yu Yuan Garden. Her backpack purse left her hands free to photograph. She shot the shiny Oriental Pearl Tower rising above the dragon roof of the garden entrance. She would call it "Shanghai, Old and New." She would not think of Jack, and his near-dawn appearance.

By the Nine-Corner Bridge, a woman convulsed. Her eyes were clamped shut and her limbs were shaking. She was either very ill or practicing a martial art, and it was hard for Karla not to stare—she was tempted to take a picture, but didn't.

Karla strolled on. It was a lovely spring day, cool and bright. Clear air, if not clean. Little bridges, little pagodas.

Tower of Returning Clouds, Tower for Beholding the Moon, Three Ears of Corn Hall.

Jack had come back at 4:13 A.M. The Texan doctor had invited him out. He was too pissed to leave a note, he said.

At the Pavilion for Viewing Frolicking Fish, a group of gangly teenage boys lounged in their school uniforms. They moved as though they weren't wearing ties and jackets, as though their teacher hadn't escorted them there. The more courageous ones, with chin stubble, pointed at Karla and smirked.

Jack would have pointed back, or picked his nose, or danced the hornpipe. Karla ignored them, nobly, and they ceased to exist.

Jack had reeked of cigarettes when he came in, and of vodka.

She concentrated on the murky pond water, the fat goldfish. She squinted and made everything blurry. *Rookeries,* she thought. Had she made this word up? She meant the jagged rocks placed artfully, sparingly, for no apparent reason.

Men spit deeply. The phlegm buckets, positioned throughout the garden, were disregarded.

She knew exactly where he'd gone. The Gotham Bar. Sam had told her about it. There were pretty girls you could talk to in close booths. A touristy thing, nothing more. Just talking. They spoke good English there. It was something for the expats to do.

Tower for Watching Waves, Hall of Mildness, Tower of Joy, Tower of Vitality, Hall of Jade Magnificence.

Jack said, "I couldn't really say no. And you weren't in the room." His voice was thin, raspy. He'd been talking all night, loudly. He wanted only to sleep.

She let him sleep, and couldn't herself. Her stomach felt vast, inflated—air, veggie buns. She got up long before he did and left a note. Tonight they would wear red.

At the Hall of Nine Lions, a wet rag had been flung over a railing. A flyswatter had been propped against a stone. Mops and brooms, stuffed in corners. The nooks and crannies claimed by the cleaners.

Karla blocked out the flyswatter and it, too, ceased to exist. (Tower of Lasting Clearness, Hall of Heralding Spring.) *Zap*. Spittoons, phlegm—*zap*. She used an entire roll of film, and this seemed right. She obeyed the exit sign, in English.

She was two yuan short of the taxi fare back to the hotel, but the driver was forgiving. "It's okay," he said, and she thanked him in his language and hurried back into the lobby.

Tonight they would to have smile next to each other again, song after song.

SIX

Celine Dion

WILLOW STOOD NEXT TO Karla at the bar and said, "My house. You want to come? Ten A.M., hotel lobby. We'll learn the Chinese song. Maybe dumplings. Jack, too."

"Yes," said Karla, before thinking. A distraction, a day away. And dumplings. Jack wouldn't come.

"Day off tomorrow," Willow explained.

"Good. Yes."

Willow's house was in Pudong, across the river. It was the lesser Shanghai, said the guidebook. Not the suburbs, but the other side of the tracks.

"I'm going to Willow's house," Karla announced in the room, brushing her teeth.

"What?"

She spit and rinsed. "Willow's house. I'm going tomorrow."

He waited. She didn't invite him.

"Have fun," he said. "Tell her I'm sleeping. Tell her I'm a lazy fuck and I didn't want to get out of bed. And that I hate Chinese people to boot."

Drunkard. She itched to say it out loud. "It's a girl day," she said. "You'd be bored. We're going to do our nails."

He tossed a bottle in the direction of the tiny pail and missed.

At 10:20 Karla peeked outside to see Willow pacing by the hotel street entrance. She was dressed in white and black checked trousers, a soft white blouse, and a green chiffon scarf carefully knotted at her throat. Her shoes were tan and suede and had cost two thousand yuan. Willow would tell her, later—a new gift from Mr. Marcello, her Italian boyfriend. Karla wore jeans and Converse sneakers, recently pristine and now gray from Shanghai streets.

"*Outside,* not inside," said Willow. "Hotel staff not allowed inside on off day."

"I didn't realize. I didn't see you out here—"

"Where Jack?"

"Sick." *From beer.* "Not feeling well." *Farting in ways that are not healthy for any human being.* Karla clutched her stomach to illustrate sickness. "He's sleeping." She made the universal sleeping sign (head tilted into hands at prayer). Willow knew these words, but Karla couldn't help herself.

"No problem," said Willow. "You and me." She raised her hand and a cab instantly slowed.

The fog lifted, and steel cranes—vague yellow monsters, multiplying—appeared from below. Karla saw two, then four, then a dozen—metal things rising up and moving, inching along. They were surrounded.

Willow touched the sleeve of Karla's jean jacket. "Calvin Klein?"

"I'm not sure," said Karla. Kmart, actually.

"I like." She opened her purse and pressed a Dairy Milk into Karla's palm. "You like?"

"Yes. Chocolate." So easy. Brand names and candy. The meter was clicking. Willow spoke to the taxi driver for several minutes, and he smiled a little in return.

The meter stopped at 47. "Fifty yuan, Ka-la," said Willow. She sat back sweetly and waited. The cabbie waited. The bus, Karla knew, was two yuan, for a one-hour ride. Kara paid, and outside it was sheer bright daylight. The neighbors stared.

Willow's home was on the fifth floor of a dark concrete building. The cement steps were swept, and as they climbed Karla saw slippers on each doormat, waiting for feet.

On Willow's doormat, there were three pairs. "Look! Small shoes for you, big shoes for Jack!" She slid off her suede flats and rubbed away an invisible smudge. She opened the metal gate, then the door.

The apartment was only slightly larger than Karla and Jack's hotel room, complete with living room, kitchen, bedroom, and bathroom. Everything was clean and dusted—the wooden floors, the lace cloths over tables and chairs. Karla could see her breath. She kept her coat on, and Willow led her to the bedroom, which she apparently shared with her mother. *She's a teenager,* Karla realized. She had treasures on display: a folded quilt with tiny red hearts, bright stuffed animals (a bear from Mr. Marcello and a tiger from a hotel staff party), a small desk with a large lamp, a wooden vanity table with pictures under a pane of glass.

Willow tapped the glass. "This is mother." The photograph looked brittle and the woman was tall, with sharp cheekbones and a square chin—a less delicate Willow. She worked at the Pudong Tower, the gift shop, and would be there all day, on a twelve-hour shift. "One day work, one day off," Willow explained.

Willow tapped another picture, a man in a hammock. "This is father." She spoke quickly, and Karla knew what was coming. "But he is gone already."

Next was the living room, where Willow had placed little paper bags of sweets on the table: more Dairy Milks, pistachios, and little tubs of Jell-O. "You try," said Willow, and deftly squirted a Jell-O pod into Karla's mouth. It was lime, and squishy. Karla wanted another.

Willow had moved on to the TV, which was much larger than the one in Karla and Jack's room. It looked brand-new. "VCD and VCR," Willow explained.

"I think Celine Dion," she decided, and played "Because You Loved Me" three times. She asked Karla to sing it, which Karla did, quietly. She hated the song. She had to stop for a moment to clear her throat of Jell-O. Willow watched Karla's mouth and sang along, too. Willow had a thin, sweet voice, and good pitch. Karla told her so.

"I know this. I can be singer. I like song high."

"Yes, this song is very high."

"Yes, I like."

Her other two CDs were by a male singer from Hong Kong. "Very famous," she said. "You want a drink?" She retrieved two cans of apple juice and played a song by the Hong Kong guy. *"Hold tight my lady! Hold tight my lady!"* he sang. This seemed to be the chorus. It was the only part Karla understood.

"You like?"

Karla nodded. "You have any more pictures, Willow?" She did, but not of Mr. Marcello. Karla wanted to see him.

"They all in *his* room!" Willow said, laughing. His room *where*? In the hotel? In Shanghai? Did she stay there often?

They looked at other pictures, of Willow in pigtails, Willow on a swing set, Willow holding a puppy ("I like this dog so much!" she remembered), Willow with relatives. "This my uncle," she said, pointing to a little girl. In all her class pictures she was the tallest and prettiest, by far. There were very few pictures of her father.

Willow finished her apple juice and said that it was time.

"Time to learn Chinese song. Slow song or quick song?" Slow would be easier. Willow retrieved a large tape deck from the bedroom and the lesson began.

"Too ran jhan eye knee..."

Karla wrote the lines phonetically on a blank sheet of paper. "What does it mean?"

"Love song," said Willow. "I don't know." She pressed Pause, sang the line on her own, then told Karla to repeat each phrase. Willow knew every nuance, every breath of this song, and she wasn't tired of hearing it.

Then she left Karla in the living room, to practice, while she made lunch.

Karla pretended to study but instead watched Willow through the low archway separating the rooms. Willow stirred a sticky white paste until it smelled like fried dough and scrambled eggs with yellow spices. ("I like egg," she called out. "You like?") There were persistent sizzling noises from the oil in the wok. There was soy sauce in small bowls, mixed with something from a red bottle.

"Eat," Willow said, and Karla turned off the tape player and sat at the table, as directed. The dumplings slipped from her chopsticks and Willow laughed and Karla thought of the

Robin Williams movie where his girlfriend loved dumplings but could never hold them properly—it was much too hard to explain all this. Willow touched Karla's wrist and told her to hold the chopsticks in a different way. They ate until Karla felt greasy and full.

Willow looked around for something, and found it. "From Mr. Marcello. He buys it in Australia, on business," she said, and uncoiled a silver tube of orange lipstick. Mr. Marcello did something important for an Italian restaurant chain, but Willow didn't know what, exactly.

The lipstick was perfect, untouched, and Karla brought the new matte tip to her lips without thinking. Willow's eyes flashed a little, but Karla couldn't stop herself—the lipstick glided on beautifully, silkily, unlike the cheap, chalky stuff she used, reds and pinks that blotched and stained. She closed the cap, rubbed her lips together, tasting plastic and something like oranges. *Sorry,* she thought, but she didn't feel particularly sorry.

Willow said nothing for several seconds and then, "I style you."

"Yes," said Karla, and Willow's fingers were in her hair, combing it slowly. The Hong Kong singer was on the VCD again, wearing a purple shirt unbuttoned two buttons too many. He was on a beach, his pant legs wet. He looked very sad.

Karla twisted away to face the TV, and Willow twisted her back again, gently, in order to reach her hair.

"There, Ka-la." Willow clicked off the singer so Karla could see her reflection in the blank TV: startled face, framed by a French braid. Karla told Willow what it was called.

"We call this 'twiss,'" Willow said. "I like."

"I like," Karla repeated.

And then Willow jerked her hand through the braid, unraveling it all.

She put Karla's hair in a ballet bun, as Karla sometimes did when her hair wasn't washed.

"I *don't* like," said Willow. "You look like grandmother." Her fingers were holding the bun in place, and she asked Karla to stand up, nudging her to the vanity mirror in the bedroom.

"My friends always wanted to do this, growing up," Karla said. "I never let them." Willow nodded at Karla's talking mouth in the mirror. She was studying the color on Karla's lips.

And still Willow's hand was there, holding the bun in place, touching the base of Karla's neck—her hand, that was all, but Karla could sense the length of her, her height, her slimness.

"I think outside," said Willow. She dropped her hand and Karla's hair fell. "Sunny day now." Through the bedroom window the buildings looked inches apart, and everywhere it was washing day—the stoops and fire escapes were filled with hanging clothes. Karla was shivering a little. She'd abandoned her coat when they ate—it had seemed the polite thing to do. Willow pushed open the window, and the air outside was warm, a great relief.

"We walk," Willow decided. At the door she put on her suede shoes and Karla folded her single sheet of Chinese lyrics and they were off.

Karla sang in the stairwell. *"Doo-ron John eye knee."* She *felt* like singing, and the echo in the corridor was hollow and pleasing.

On the street there was more staring, and Willow seemed pleased. She tightened the scarf knot at her neck and held Karla's hand firmly. They passed sooty guardrails and the concrete shell of a condominium. A barefoot man tried to sell them a brown leather belt from a loop of dozens around his neck. A giant mound of plastic bottles wheeled itself by, miraculously bundled, balanced, and strapped to the back of a bicycle. The sun warmed Karla's bones, and she was happy to walk, her lips pretty, her stomach full.

Karla remembered walking in Costa Smeralda during a day off from the ship. They were docked three miles from the town, at the very end of a straight, flat road, and she had hiked the length of it with Holly and Serena to a restaurant, just to go somewhere. They sang "Wonderwall" and got the words all wrong, and the ship seemed far away. She couldn't remember where Jack had been that day, but she hadn't minded his absence.

Willow sang "Because You Loved Me" and "Slow Hand," and Karla changed the lyrics to "I wanna man with a *Marcello* hand," and Willow grinned. Karla sang the Chinese song again. She had to sing it by herself, Willow said. For practice.

They passed a small stream with more garbage than water. "Very dirty," said Willow. She untied her scarf, warming up now, folded it several times, and put it in her little white purse. (She had to drop Karla's hand to do this, but she grabbed it again when she was done.) Her feet hurt, she said. She was getting blisters from her new shoes. Her palm was moist and hot.

"What size feet?" Willow asked.

Karla told her, looking down at her big, dirty sneakers. Was that still important here?

"Mr. Marcello say I have small feet."

"Has your mother met Mr. Marcello?"

"Met? Yes. My mother has met. Mother is forty-three. Mr. Marcello is forty-five. He my *father,* she say. I say, not father, *boy*friend!"

"Does she like him?"

"Yes, she like. But not just his money. She like *him.*"

"She doesn't think Mr. Marcello is too old for you?" Karla squeezed Willow's hand a little, so the question wouldn't seem rude, and Willow squeezed back.

"Not old! I like Mr. Marcello!"

"What does he look like?"

"Like Italian man."

They passed a group of boys throwing sticks at a wire fence. "You like children?" Karla asked.

"No. Mr. Marcello like."

They'd talked about kids?

"I like baby," said Willow. "Very small. Not like this." She pointed to the kids. "You like?"

"I like, but not now. Later. Maybe in five years or so." *In five years,* Karla noted, *I'll be thirty.*

"I think three years," said Willow.

"You want children in three years?"

"Yes. No. I don't know."

They entered the Lotus Supermarket, which looked like Kmart. There were signs in English: "The low prices. For YOU!" Willow touched a giant stuffed tiger ("Jack like?"), inquired about the price of lipstick, then led Karla back out into the gray.

She checked Karla's watch. It was 2:00 P.M. "Very sleepy," she said. "I go home and you go home," she said.

Karla agreed, although she wasn't in a rush. She thought of Jack in his squash clothes.

"Palace!" Willow ordered, as a cab slowed. Then she limped away, waving, shining in all her white, pausing to rub her blistered heels.

SEVEN

The Carpenters

FOR EASTER THE reception desk was lined with head-size plaster eggs. There was a small corral by the revolving glass doors with fake green grass and real live bunnies. Karla lingered there. She wanted to pick them up and scoot them through the revolving doors. She wanted to set the bunnies free. A hot air balloon floated above the Continental Café, rainbow-striped, and chocolate lambs were on display at Gourmet Corner.

"Special Easter Menu," Jack said at dinner. He wore his fake Armani suit, from Dubai. Everything else was still in Laundry. He wore the watch Karla had bought him in Saint Martin, after he'd given her the bracelet. In the Caribbean the watch had looked cheerful and decadent: fake gold with one large, real emerald on the face. It was too tight for his wrist now.

Karla kept an eye on the rabbits, across the lobby. Well-dressed Chinese children at nearby tables looked longingly, too.

"I recommend the rabbit stew," said Jack. He sipped his

allotted glass of chardonnay. (They weren't allowed to order bottles with dinner anymore.) Jack's pinkie was raised. His green stone winked.

THAT NIGHT, Karla began to experiment with cabaret gestures—jazz hands, finger snaps. The bar was dead and Willow was off. They had three sets left to go. Karla was trying to decide if small dance steps would work, just easy ones. Kick, ball change. Pivot step.

Jack gave her a long, curious look.

During the break they sat and stared at the lights below and sipped the Imperial White they'd brought up in Evian bottles. Jack put a cigarette in the fist of the kneeling Buddha statue.

"We *have* to stay until September?" said Karla. "We can't ask to leave sooner?"

Jack didn't answer. He said, "Buy your own, you cheap bastard." He was talking to Buddha.

KARLA USED THE ladies' room in Xian Court, three floors below the Sky Bar, just to go somewhere new. A Chinese woman played a traditional Chinese stringed thing there, nightly. A zither? No. Karla had known the name once. She'd had to memorize it for her World Music exam. The class was also known as Clapping for Credit, and this had been apt.

If Karla's World Music professor had been there, he would have had a conversation with the zither player, in Mandarin. He would have asked if he could have a go. He spoke five languages. He smoked pot before class, or that was the rumor. He wore parachute pants with zippers and floral-print shirts.

Karla hadn't spoken to the zither woman yet, or the Filipino jazz trio in the lobby, or the Russian string quartet in the Continental Café. But then again, they hadn't spoken to her.

"We don't have any friends here," Karla said to Jack, back in the Sky Bar.

"Where did you go?"

"Xian Court."

"Exciting? Was the violinist there?"

"It's not a violin. I was saying, we don't have friends."

"Willow, Margaret, Sam—what are they?"

"But we don't really see them often, outside of work."

"You mean non-Chinese friends."

"No, I mean people we can socialize with. I mean drinking buddies."

"Sam drinks like a fish."

"You know what I mean."

They hadn't heard from the Muscat duos. Karla had sent postcards weeks ago. They'd renewed their contracts, surely—Milk and Honey and Double Speak. They were probably poolside now, drinking screwdrivers.

"We should make an effort," Karla said. "We should go listen to other bands and make friends."

"Since when are we a band?"

AS THOUGH conjured, the duo from Yangzi Suites appeared. Karla recognized them from the ad in the *Shanghai Star.* They were both curvy with dyed blond hair. They sat in the middle of the room—not too close and not too far away—and they listened without commenting to each other, though Karla suspected they wanted to. Jack and Karla played their strongest numbers, starting with "Lean on Me" and ending with "Smooth Operator."

"Yangzi Suites duo," Willow confirmed, between songs. "Want to buy you a drink." And to Karla, "Her hair—bad color. Not good with her skin."

They were called Gin Fizz, G for Glo and F for Flynn. Glo wore a crisp, tan pantsuit, and her handshake was incredibly strong. Flynn was shorter, with gray creeping in at his temples. G and F also stood for Great Britain and Finland, they said. Flynn was Finnish, although he now had a perfect Midlands accent.

"I like 'Killing Me Softly,' " Glo announced.

Flynn nodded. "Not an easy song to sing!"

"We do it," said Jack. He was on his second cigarette in ten minutes.

"She plays, you see," Flynn explained, meaning piano, meaning Glo.

Glo shrugged. "We both play. We both sing."

"Yours is the best," Flynn added. His hands were fluttering over his lighter, his straw. "The best bar, clearly. Yes? You've seen the others? Ritz-Carlton? Marriott?" They had to play in the Yangzi Suites lobby, he said, next to several enormous potted plants.

"We have to go back," Jack announced, checking his watch. They promised to come to the Yangzi on their night off.

Jack cued "Killing Me Softly," and Karla sang. It wasn't her best version, but she got the verses out in the right order. She did the Fugee thing where she usually did the Roberta Flack thing, and she caught Flynn nodding in recognition. They left a few songs later, during "Every Breath You Take," just before Jack's guitar solo.

"Maybe they'll be our friends," Karla said, as Jack changed discs.

"He's a wanker," said Jack.

✧

INSTEAD OF GOING to Yangzi Suites to see Gin Fizz on their night off, they went to a new place in the French Quarter, called Milo's Bar. The building had small columns with floral details. Corinthian, Karla remembered.

At Milo's they met Charles, a pianist from New Orleans who played six nights a week. Charles had a daughter in Shanghai, and a tiny apartment just ten minutes away by bike. The girl's mother had a new boyfriend now, also American, and they all got along. Charles sometimes brought his daughter to Milo's. She was five and liked Beatles songs, of which Charles knew many.

This was all revealed during Charles's fifteen-minute break.

The next week Charles appeared at the Sky Bar, denim-clad. He drank Guinness and showed them his ticket stub from the Forever Pleasure Hall of Paradise Palace movie theater. *Titanic* was playing—they should go. The tickets were cheap, and the Chinese subtitles were unobtrusive. The Chinese Cultural Bureau had approved the film because it confirmed the dangers of capitalism, Charles explained. All those crystal table settings on a ship doomed to sink. All that fuss over a fat blue diamond necklace.

"We'll go," Karla said. "Definitely." She wanted a ticket stub.

Charles asked Jack to write down the chords to "Get Back," which Jack did, on a gold Sky Bar napkin.

Charles looked like Lyle Lovett, Karla decided. Odd and big-nosed, but gentle. Comfortable in his oddness. He'd never hurt you, if you could stand that kind of thing.

"What kind of thing?" asked Jack. Karla was explaining her theory out loud, after Charles had left.

"Niceness. Complete lack of cynicism."

"I'm nice," Jack said.

"You are," said Karla. *You can be.* "But you have a sense of humor."

"I like to think so."

"You're not *too* nice."

"I get it. You said that already."

"Which is why I'll never understand the Julia Roberts debacle."

He ignored this last word. "People make mistakes."

"Strange, though. I wonder if it was real, or if she was just testing herself, seeing how long she could do it."

"She married the guy. Kind of an extreme test, don't you think?"

"People get married all the time, for all kinds of reasons."

"Deep," said Jack, and deftly changed the subject.

"to me," jack said much later, in bed, "Easter is about eggs. Not bunnies or chickens or jelly beans—that's so American. It's just eggs: Cadbury eggs, Mars eggs, Bounty eggs. They'll be in the shops at home now." It was 3:00 a.m., and Karla was tired. Jack wasn't. His birthday was soon, he reminded her. His breath smelled like vodka.

"I used to get loads of chocolate eggs for my birthday. One from Mam, one from Grampa, one from my auntie Peg—"

"Who isn't your real aunt."

"No. And I'd steal Duncan's egg on Easter morning, before he woke up."

"That's terrible," said Karla. Her eyes were closed. She tried to imagine a ten-year-old Jack. "Did you steal Liam's egg, too?" His brothers were both in Yorkshire, both married. They looked nothing at all like Jack.

"No, just Dunc's." And Karla knew why, without asking. Because Duncan would have laughed about it and Liam would have cried. Jack was a good brother that way.

"Did you decorate eggs? Real eggs?" If she'd had the energy, Karla would have described the pellets of dissolving dye and the little cardboard holders for the eggs and the designs she drew in crayon (hearts, peace signs, lightning bolts) before dipping the eggs in glasses of pink and green and yellow water. The water seeped through the flimsy cardboard egg rack and stained the countertop, but this never seemed to bother Karla's mom. Karla would be bothered, she knew, by the stains and spills children made.

"Too girlie," said Jack. "I didn't decorate." But his mom and Liam had. "Then I'd roll them down the road and wait for them to be run over by cars."

"That's such a boy thing to do," said Karla. "We ate our eggs. For a week after Easter I took egg salad sandwiches to school."

He didn't say anything else, and so Karla rested her head in his armpit, and that was enough. They wouldn't have sex and they wouldn't have to feel guilty because they'd talked about Easter eggs instead.

———

THE NEXT NIGHT, Jack returned from Fast Snack at 2:13 A.M. and said that one of the bunnies was trying to escape through a gap in the pen.

"You should have helped it," said Karla.

"It might get hurt out there," Jack said. Karla imagined the bunny hopping around the slick, cold marble floors of the lobby and shitting by the reception desk. It didn't seem too dangerous.

"What do you think will happen to them after Easter?"

Jack crawled into bed and sighed. "We're all merely shadows." He'd been reading an overpriced paperback from the Palace gift shop called *Tunnel at the End of the Light*.

JACK'S BIRTHDAY arrived. They would celebrate the night before, on their night off. Karla bought an egg for him, a fancy chocolate one sprinkled with almonds and wrapped in cellophane and silk flowers, from Gourmet Corner.

She ironed and tried on three dresses, then chose a skirt.

They ate at Fast Snack, because it was free, and as she waited for her steamed vegetable buns to arrive, Karla caught him staring.

"What?"

"You look nice." He hadn't said that in a while. She felt nice. Festive. They had tickets to see *Titanic* and people to see later on (Gin Fizz, plus Charles), and she had presents to give him in the morning, hidden in the closet (bottle of Absolut, Crazy Driver! CD-ROM, Double Stuf Oreos, sent from home).

When they stumbled back to the room at 6:00 A.M., the street was quiet and the light was new and pale. Karla walked in a reasonably straight line.

"Do we need any water?" she asked. The 24 Hour Buy Store beckoned.

"I don't know," Jack said, and steered her through the revolving doors.

In the afternoon, she snuck out to buy the final birthday things: wrapping paper, bows, Coke to mix with Absolut. She made him hide in the bathroom while she lit the candles.

When he came out and saw it all, he coughed. "Busy little beaver," he said, and squeezed her elbow, her closest body part. They cracked open the vodka—it was a special occasion—and Jack spent the rest of the day plowing red monster trucks into blue monster trucks on his laptop.

After work, after they were tucked in safely together in beige sheets, he said, "You've been so nice to me."

She thought he meant always, these past three and a half years.

"My birthday's over. I guess you can go back to being miserable." He laughed, to take away the sting, and Karla made herself laugh, too.

✧

SONNY THE BLUES MAN and Wanda, his lady friend, showed up next at the Sky Bar. Both were hairy and American. Sonny, bearded, wore dark sunglasses, and Wanda clutched a long Guatemalan shawl.

"We've come to check you out," said Wanda. "Charles sent us." They sat right in front.

"Don't people in your country have access to razors?" Jack whispered to Karla.

Sonny had been called "an expert blues guy" in the *Shanghai Star*, and so Jack refused to play anything with guitar solos. During their break Karla talked to her and Jack to him.

"Great voice," Wanda began, and Karla warmed to her instantly.

"I'm very old," Wanda said. "Forty-seven. Shocker, isn't it?"

It was. Her skin was smooth, and her eyes were a very bright blue. She was a recent divorcée, she said, after twenty-five years of marriage. They'd tried and tried and nearly killed each other in the process. And now she taught at a private school in Pudong. Her family thought she was nuts, but she had to *do* something. She had to get as far away as possible.

Tipsy, lonely words spilled out. Karla felt very tired suddenly. She tapped Jack's kneecap under the table, and he tapped back.

As for Sonny, Wanda explained, he worked for Bank of America during the day and played three nights a week in three different bars, for no money.

"He's a wannabe," she said, in a stage whisper. "*And* he's in love with me. He speaks Chinese and he's been in Shanghai for ages. He takes me everywhere." Sonny pretended not to hear.

When the break was over they played "Black Magic Woman" followed by "Layla" followed by "Little Wing." Jack had turned up his amp.

THE FOLLOWING Saturday, after work, they went to see Sonny at Chamber, a blues bar above a neon nightclub. Chamber had velvet couches and thick brocade curtains and shelves lined with candles. "Paisley Park," said Karla. She'd seen a photo in *Rolling Stone* once. But Jack couldn't hear. The thud of bass speakers rattled up from the dance club below.

"Oh dear," said Karla. Sonny played keyboards to a drum machine and sang in a gravelly voice. There were a dozen people in the bar, and only Jack and Karla clapped. There was nothing remotely bluesy about him.

"Be nice to him," said Jack. "He's deluded."

After his set, Sonny delivered his monologue. Half an hour passed, then forty minutes, and no one told him to get up and start playing again. Jack plied him with drinks, and by the end of the hour Sonny was wheezing with self-congratulatory laughter. He continued to wear his ridiculous sunglasses. *Fucking Jerry Garcia and David Crosby and every aging hairy rocker in existence.* Karla was sipping and sipping because no one was speaking to her. Lift the glass, swallow; it was something to do with her hands.

And then, at last, the yuan were dispensed and they were free to go. Jack had to remind Karla to take her purse.

✧

IN CHINA, Willow explained, a baby was nine months old when it was born. So Willow was really nineteen, not eighteen.

"Life begins at conception," said Karla. "Some people believe that in America, too."

"In America, I am Cancer," said Willow.

"And here you are a Monkey," said Karla.

"Yes, Monkey."

Karla was a Rat. She knew this because of the paper place mats in China-By-The-Sea, back home. She couldn't remember what Jack was. A Bull? Something like a bull.

"Monkey is better than Cancer. Not a disease."

Karla agreed.

"Cheery talk," said Jack, appearing. "I'm a Snake."

"You're not," said Karla.

"I am. Year of the Snake."

"Snake is cold animal," said Willow. "You eat the snake when you are hot."

"Karla shouldn't eat it then," said Jack. "She's cold enough already."

"What's that supposed to mean?" said Karla.

"Nothing. You're always cold. You always want a sweater."

Go on, say it, Karla thought. *Frigid.*

✧

JACK, OVER DINNER, told Karla he used to sell foam. Not Styrofoam or camera case foam, but the kind of foam in furniture. There were many different plies and thicknesses, and he would often have to try out new products in the warehouse and report back to his bosses. There was something called the Initial Sit, which was the first impression, sitting down. The initial impact of foam on ass.

"So how did you describe it?" Karla asked. "'Really soft'? 'Really, really soft'?"

"No." He ignored her tone. "We had a scale, from one to ten, ten being the best."

"Did you ever find a ten?"

He thought for a moment, took a drag. "I don't think so. A few eights and nines."

Karla was trying not to drink tonight, and so she kept asking questions. What were his bosses like? Did they joke about the Initial Sit?

"No, it was serious. It was business."

"But you're talking about asses on foam. It's funny."

"It was my job." He stubbed his Marlboro in the gold ashtray; he stubbed into the *y* of *Sky Bar*.

"You brought it up," Karla said.

"It popped into my head. Forget it."

✧

THAT NIGHT AN American named Cy tipped them a hundred dollars each because they played "Hello Mary Lou," his favorite song.

"Tonight my whole teenage years were just, you know, brought back to life," said Cy, after their last set. His eyes were watery. He wore a checked shirt and a chunky diamond ring, which he slipped on and off as he spoke. He was from Iowa. He'd met his wife when he was fifteen and she was thirteen. They'd been together ever since.

"No complaints?" asked Jack.

"Oh no." Cy chuckled. "Not on my part, at least."

Cy was in window decor. "Venetian blinds," he said, "window quilts, that sort of thing."

Karla said, "My parents have window quilts in their house," and then wished she hadn't. She squeezed the hundred-dollar bill into her palm. She had no pockets.

Cy was celebrating because he'd just supplied blinds to the new Thistle Hotel on Nanjing Lu.

Jack said, "We'll get this round," and Karla thought, *Why?* And Jack answered, "You'd have to be a millionaire to celebrate properly in *this* bar!"

Cy paused and smiled, and Karla begged, *Don't say it, don't say it,* but Cy said it. "I *am* a millionaire, actually."

Jack forced himself not to look at Karla. "Well, then," he said. "Cheers."

The conversation turned to *Titanic,* which Cy didn't want to see. Cy was a *Titanic* buff. He'd read all the books and seen some documentaries, and he just knew the film would make it all seem trivial.

"And I know just what will happen in the end," he said. He wasn't smiling when he said this. Jack restrained himself admirably.

"We used to work on a ship," said Karla. "We saw it, the movie. I'd give it a B."

"B plus," said Jack.

Willow appeared behind the bar and looked at Karla, and then at her watch. The bar would close in five minutes, and Cy had just ordered another round. Karla shrugged. *What can I do?*

Willow frowned and turned away. She'd had a hard night. A guest had yelled at her because Jack hadn't played "Moon River."

"MILLIONAIRE," said Jack, in the elevator, after Cy had finally gone.

"From blinds," Karla added. *Like foam,* she thought, but didn't say.

✧

LITTLE WOMEN was on TV, after work. They undressed, and Jack said, "I feel fat."

"Shut up and watch *Little Women,*" said Karla.

"If they called it *Fat Women,* maybe I could watch it." He

slept, and snored, and Karla watched the film. She cried when Beth died. And Jo—writing so much by hand! Just paper and pen and her fingers doing all the work—how cramped and satisfying it looked. Up to her wrist in ink and Claire Danes as her sister.

It reminded Karla of the hours she'd spent singing scales in practice rooms in college—the piano pocked with cigarette burns, the thin pages of her discount music books. Jazz standards, Joni Mitchell.

She slept easily, inspired.

✧

THEY WENT TO SEE *Titanic* again at the Forever Pleasure Hall of Paradise Palace, which still smelled like urine and stale popcorn.

It was better the second time around. The corny lines didn't bother Karla as much. She was beginning to think Leonardo DiCaprio *was* cute.

"I don't want it to sink this time," Jack said, near the end, reaching for her hand.

She squeezed back. When they left they were both a little teary. The ship was so pretty before it crumbled—real wood, real chandeliers, real instruments played by martyred musicians.

SATURDAY NIGHT they returned from their break to find fourteen requests for "My Heart Will Go On." They hadn't bothered to learn it yet, although it had now officially replaced "Candle in the Wind" as the number one Sky Bar request. Jack usually said something like "Sorry, we don't know this song, but here's another Celine Dion ballad for your listening pleasure."

Tonight he said, "We've had some requests during the break." He used his microphone voice. "I'd just like to read them out to you:

> *Celine Dion, "My Heart Will Go On."*
> *Celine Dion, "My Heart Will Go On."*
> *"My Heart Will Go On."*
> Titanic *song, Celine Dion.*

Willow came up to the stage with a grin and handed him two more.

"'My Heart Will Go On,' Celine Dion, *and* Celine Dion, 'My Heart Will Go On.'"

Jack looked at Karla for a moment and then continued.

"Look, I don't know if someone's having a laugh or what, but we don't do the song. We *don't!*"

A Chinese man stood up near the back. "We want '*Ti-tanic*'!"

"You can't *have* '*Titanic*'!" said Karla. It felt good to speak. "You can have 'Under the Boardwalk,' though."

"We'll try our best to learn it," Jack cut in. "We'll be here until September, so those of you who come here often will hear it before then. And those of you who are just passing through…"

Karla could see him deciding—

"Too bad."

She let out a nervous bark of laughter.

"We *do* have an extensive song list," he continued, "and this is available from the lovely Willow."

Willow beamed.

"Please realize that there are an infinitesimal number of songs in the world"—he was pleased he'd said it right—"and we can't possibly know every one."

(She didn't bother correcting him.)

"Sorry, Kar. We have to do it," he whispered off mike. "So this evening you won't be hearing the *Titanic* song 'My Heart Will Go On,' by Celine Dion, but we will certainly do our very best to learn it in the near future." Cue for "Power of Love," in a key that wasn't Karla's best, and for the next forty-five minutes the bar was rapt.

"No one understand what you're saying," said Willow, during the break. "Crazy boy, talking, talking. They just want *'Titanic.'* They think you say you're going to play *'Titanic.'* Easy song. I know this song." And she began to sing.

In the morning Karla went to the bootleg CD stall across from the Jing'An Temple and bought the soundtrack. She wrote out the words. She could hit everything until the key change, at which point she would ask Jack to fade out. The applause would thunder and absorb her lack. She would bow, deeply.

EIGHT

Ike and Tina

In THE MORNING Karla left Jack at his desk in his boxer shorts and walked back to the Jing'An Temple. She paid her two yuan and passed under the yellow arch. Just inside, a blind man rattled the change in his paper cup. He'd been at 24 Hour the day before. How blind was he?

There were four small buildings inside the temple gates, each painted yellow, each with a large central statue of Buddha. People were waving great handfuls of incense sticks, and chunks of incense burned in large pots. The air was thick and sweet with the smell of ash and cinnamon. Karla liked the Buddhas, their shiny roundness, and she considered kneeling—why not? Jack wasn't there. But there were monks with shaved heads in black cloaks, singing and striking things with mallets. They might think she was mocking them.

She retraced her steps and turned east on Nanjing Lu. She wasn't ready to go back to all the beige.

She stopped at Heaven Café because it looked small and cheerful with its bright blue awning. She supposed she could read there for a while. A Chinese man jumped from his seat as she entered and said, "I am Steve. Do you want to eat?"

Karla said no, just a cup of cocoa, please.

"American?"

She said yes, and Steve seemed very pleased and pointed to two men in the café who were also American. Karla nodded and sat at a table far away from them, by the window. Karen Carpenter crooned, and the Americans spoke to each other (visas, movies, a new restaurant near the Bund). It was an eavesdropping kind of place. She liked it. She pretended to read and peed twice.

When Karla paid her bill, the cashier asked what had brought her to Shanghai.

"I sing at the Sky Bar," she said, and the woman squealed and led Karla back to her table. She said she'd very much like to buy Karla a drink.

"Sky Bar! I like your music very much! My name is Tammy." Karla ordered a lager and lime, because it was listed on the chalkboard in big letters, and Tammy explained that she wanted to "make friends with all the singers in the world." She used to sing Chinese songs, she said, but singing wasn't steady enough, and so she and her husband, Steve, had bought the café together. She mentioned the Hard Rock Cafe band, and Sonny the Blues Man, and Charles from Milo's— and anytime Jack and Karla came in they could have happy hour prices. Karla said thank you, that was very kind, and Tammy said don't forget, they were open till 5:00 A.M.

"We name the place after the Bryan Adams song 'Heaven.' You know this?"

"Yes."

"But Sky Bar is very beautiful."

"But not very lively," said Karla.

Tammy agreed.

Karla finished her pint and Tammy offered another.

"No, I need to practice," Karla said, although this was a lie. Tammy escorted her to the door and waved, and Karla walked back to the hotel quickly, anxious to tell Jack, anxious to pee again.

Jack was at the computer. "Are you drunk?"

Was it obvious? She was smiling widely. "I made a friend," she said. She waited. She could see him deciding whether or not to be jealous.

He decided. "We're not allowed." He hit Save, and the disc drive whirred. "No friends allowed." Karla's stomach rippled slightly with relief. She worried lately that he could smell the truth on her, sense her need for more people around.

"Happy hour prices," she said. "All the time."

They agreed to go after work.

✧

TAMMY AND STEVE were beaming when Jack and Karla arrived. A guy from the Hard Rock Cafe—Norm, lead guitar, from Seattle—was already there, and Tammy wheeled them to his table. "I want to make friends with every singer in the world," she said again.

"Good luck with that," said Jack. He'd lost his cigarettes. He thought someone had stolen them in the Sky Bar.

Norm wore a leather vest and spoke of his favorite foods in Shanghai: the veggie burgers at Hard Rock, the wonton soup at Fast Snack, the chicken quesadillas at Heaven.

Karla agreed with him about the wonton soup.

Norm then described his equipment, his gigs, his near studio collaboration with Steven Tyler in L.A., which fell through at the last minute, his night out with Vanessa-Mae's band when she played Shanghai. Karla nodded and Jack said little. When it was time to go, Norm shook Karla's hand for a while and slapped Jack on the shoulder and promised to come by the Sky Bar soon. Tammy and Steve stood under Heaven's awning and waved good-bye.

At last, in their room, Jack bitched about it all: the leather vest, the Steven Tyler lie.

"The drinks were cheap," Karla offered, for contrast. "That's why we went."

He lit a cigarette, right there in the room—his pack had been in his desk all along. "We went to meet North Americans," he said.

Karla ducked into the bathroom before the conversation could continue.

AN ANGULAR Chinese woman appeared at the far end of the Sky Bar the next night, and Karla watched her from the stage. She drank martinis slowly, getting quietly numb, and nodded in a solemn way when Jack sang "Unchained Melody." She smiled at Karla during the breaks, and Karla smiled back, taking note of her hat, shoes, earrings, nail polish, eye shadow, and lipstick, all in shades of green. Even her skin had an olive tint.

By the third set, the Lady in Green had company, a balding man, and they sat as close as the barstools would allow. She clasped her glass stem with Kelly-tipped fingers, and when the man spoke she nodded hard, her neck bobbing, as though this man had all the answers. It looked painful. Her spine could snap, her head could roll.

A week went by before Karla was close enough to hear. A new man had joined her, but this one wouldn't sit down. "Till one o'clock," he said, in a Boston accent. "That's forty minutes." He left, and the Lady in Green finished her drink—sweet little sips. She allowed three additional minutes to pass. She followed.

GLO FROM GIN FIZZ called at around half past one. "Come out! I've had three margaritas!" They would meet Karla and Jack at Heaven in twenty minutes.

Steve and Tammy greeted them at the door. "You look so pretty!" said Tammy.

And Jack, on cue: "Thank you."

It was beginning to bother Karla, the constant comments from Tammy and the Sky Bar girls. *I like your hair, Ka-la. I like this dress. This dress is too long for you, I think. This lipstick light, but I like. Want to try my rouge?*

And then Glo and Flynn appeared in a gust of inebriation and fleshy hugs. They'd brought along two guys from the Irish band at O'Farley's, the large, bearded fiddler and the small, jaded accordion player, whose eyes were droopy with booze. "They're the tagalongs," said Flynn. "Irish. The same damn jig over and over."

The fiddler ignored him.

"Fuck U2! Fuck Thin Lizzy!" said Flynn.

"No need to yell," Glo chirped.

"*Shhh,*" said a pale man at the bar. He caught Flynn's eye and put a bony finger to his lips.

"There's no problem," Glo said.

"Take it easy," said the pale man. "The cops will come by, I know this."

"The cops?" said Flynn.

"There's no problem," said Glo.

"The cops?" Flynn stood, and the pale man twisted to face him on his stool.

Steve stood and announced a free round for everyone. Everyone ignored Steve.

The pale man was Finnish, Glo whispered, and Flynn began to speak to him in Finnish and English, alternately.

"Who are you, anyway?" Flynn said. "Peter Fonda? Why are you wearing a *poofter* shirt?" The pale man wore a long white tunic and matching white cotton pants. His Birkenstock straps were pale blue.

But the Finn didn't bite. Instead, he explained that he wasn't Finnish, he was Chinese. He'd lived in Shanghai for twenty years and had a Chinese wife.

"That's funny," said Flynn. "Where is she then, at three in the morning? I'm with *my* wife, Jack's with *his* wife."

"We're not married," Jack said.

"Cops," said the Finn. "I promise you."

At which point Flynn pushed away his chair and spit out a long Finnish sentence.

"I will *kill* you," said the Finn, matter-of-factly, and pointed a finger at Flynn's throat.

"Fuck this finger business," said Flynn.

And with that the Finn lunged from his stool and slapped Flynn neatly on the cheek.

All the men in the bar stood up, even Jack. The fiddler cracked his knuckles. Glo began to cry.

"Why are we the only ones sitting down?" asked Karla.

Flynn held his cheek and said, "Steve. I'd like this man to leave *now!*" But the Finn didn't leave, and Steve didn't make him. Jack told Flynn to sit down.

"All I said was 'Go home, you fucking foreigner,'" Flynn told Glo. "I said this in Finnish, which is a *joke* because I'm in *China,* and *I'm* Finnish!"

"You're half Finnish," Glo said.

"I'll tell you again. All I said was 'Go back to your own country, you fucking foreigner.' Don't you see? I said this in *Finnish*—Glo, don't interrupt!—I said this in *Finnish* while in *China.* It's not an insult. How could it be?"

Glo explained: Flynn had lived in Finland until the age of fifteen, at which point a fellow Finn had called him Turkish. (Karla couldn't really see this. Dark eyebrows, slightly pudgy, a charismatic nose. But Turkish?) Now when he ran into Finns abroad, he tended to pick fights.

Jack spoke next. "That's it? You're blaming this guy for some Finn who called you a Turk, years ago?"

"That's an oversimplification, Glo. You haven't experienced the racism I have."

Glo opened her mouth and closed it again. She picked up the fiddler's drink and finished it.

And then the conversation became cyclical: current events, the slap, music, the slap, Bacardi versus Mount Gay, back to the slap. Karla stopped drinking.

"My cheek," said Flynn, again. "Is there a mark? Glo?"

"Shut up, Flynn," Jack said and, briefly, Flynn did.

The accordion player paid his bill and left. The fiddler began to shoot darts, marring the wall. The duos shared a cab to the Palace, where all but Karla decided to go to Fast Snack for sweet and sour pork. They hugged Karla good-bye in the lobby, even Jack, who would fill her in, later: Flynn borrowed money from Jack and then bossed around the waiter, the guy in the ill-fitting jacket. Jack would have to apologize to him.

But he wouldn't, Karla knew, and the guy in the ill-fitting jacket would add a hundred yuan to Jack's next Fast Snack bill, for revenge.

Meanwhile, Karla tapped toward the elevator in her clogs. A vacuum hummed in the distance. The bunnies slept soundly. It was 5:33 A.M.

THEY TOOK A TRIP to Hangzhou on their day off, because Gin Fizz had been there and liked it. There was a large lake and a few hotels with some decent bands, Glo said, and it was only an hour away. They could spend the night and take an afternoon train back and still have plenty of time for dinner before their first set.

The station platform looked like a dated movie backdrop, Karla thought, with washed-out colors and passengers hunched over shabby suitcases, actors playing contented expatriates, dealing out cards on the station floor. The conductors wore faded olive green uniforms with crooked, red epaulets.

Karla and Jack had "soft seats," with cushions, and once onboard they were given little black plastic bags for spitting. There was no AC, and Karla was wearing tight, black jeans. There were a few other Caucasian faces in their train car, all flushed, and Jack and Karla ignored them. A uniformed girl served complimentary tea in white plastic cups. Bits of green herb floated up, then sank back down.

"Nice," said Jack.

A mother and daughter sat across from them. The

mother had a pinched, wrinkled face and lips that were nearly invisible. She had tiny jade earrings in papery lobes. The daughter took out a pear and a knife and began to peel, dropping thin, neat curls of pear skin into the plastic spit bag. She cut the chunks away from the center for her mother, and chewed on the core herself.

The daughter was then free to read her paper. She hiked up her pant legs to cool off, revealing muscular calves and flesh-colored panty hose sockettes. She sat squarely, her body compact and solid, as her mother's must have been.

Jack was also watching the old lady eat the pear. He asked Karla if she had anything to eat in her purse. "We should've packed something from Gourmet Corner," he said.

"Gum," said Karla. "I have gum." Jack took a piece and chewed slowly.

The countryside appeared. Farmland. Women with hoes and hats.

"Real people," Jack said. "Backbreaking work."

Backbreaking, thought Karla. Bones, breaking—could that happen? Could a back really break that way? All those women with bones like dry sticks snapping. Grass being sliced in a hot, open field.

Karla tugged at the hairs on Jack's arm, and this was soothing, his arm hair a little damp, his shirtsleeves rolled up as far as they would go. He was solidly there, beside her, and they were moving again, traveling. They were having a small adventure.

IN HANGZHOU, they followed the crowd and waited in line at a taxi stand. An older couple stood in front of them with matching backpacks, speaking in a language that sounded like Russian. He wore khaki shorts with complicated pockets, and she wiped her neck with a fuchsia handkerchief. She was trying to read a microscopic address photocopied from Lonely Planet. "Could you?" she asked Karla, pointing to the paper, and soon the four were sharing a taxi to the Central Trade Hotel.

They were Polish but had lived in England for years. They were sixtyish and well-spoken and well-traveled; they'd lived everywhere. Karla wondered if they'd been forced to leave Poland, but it seemed rude to ask. (*Are you Jews? So am I.*)

The hotel lobby was pristine, all white, and so Jack said, "'I can still smell the fresh paint.'" He spread his arms like Kate Winslet at the bow.

The Polish couple smiled, but they hadn't seen the movie. They asked if Karla and Jack would like to meet for cocktails, say 7:00 P.M. in the hotel bar? Jack agreed and shook hands, but out of earshot he said, "Enough is enough. We know their whole bloody life story already."

"The Goodmans," said Karla. They'd registered Karla and Jack under their own passports, because Jack had forgotten theirs.

"Enough of the Goodmans, then," said Jack, and Karla felt a slight conspiratorial thrill.

In the room, Jack threw their bag on the bed and said, "You're on your hols, love!" For a second Karla thought he was going to flop down and pull her to him, but instead he went to the bathroom and sampled the free toiletries (lotion, mouthwash) without replacing the caps and then told her to hurry up, they had all of West Lake to see.

As they walked to the waterfront, people—other couples, cute children, a few lecherous men—noticed them. Boys with wet towels on their heads to cool off and girls in pastels and heels. One munched on a tiny bird, roasted whole on a stick.

Karla wanted to take a boat ride to the Three Pools Mirroring the Moon Island, in the middle of the lake. The oar man cranked the paddles of a large dinghy; his forearms bulged like Popeye's, and his face was absolutely still. On the island, they followed a path over bridges with zigzag corners. There were fat goldfish underneath the bridge, and lily pads sprinkled with one-fen coins. Jack tried three times to land one but missed. He looked happy—he hadn't smoked a cigarette in hours.

IN THE LATE afternoon they took a taxi to the opposite side of the lake. "The Stone Buddha Garden is less crowded, more scenic," Jack read. "Lots of big Buddhas, apparently." The breeze from the open window cooled them both.

They had an hour before the Garden gates closed, and so they hurried, stopping to snap photos of Buddhas reclining in various positions. They found the Laughing Buddha pictured in the guidebook, and this pleased Jack.

They napped for an hour, back at the hotel. Jack was out almost immediately, his arm flung over her chest. They showered, separately, and Karla made coffee, just to use the little packets of milk and sugar.

In the dining room, a cellist played a long, mournful version of "Somewhere Over the Rainbow," but the margaritas were lovely. They ate quickly, in order to avoid the Goodmans, and then they were back outside, where the night was balmy, tropical. Karla wasn't wearing panty hose, and all was quiet and calm outside—no traffic! At Desperado's, a "Fun

Pub," they drank more margaritas. The Filipino band was called Flower Power, and Glo and Flynn knew them, they'd said. The two girl singers, in tight jeans and halter tops, were backed by a drummer and a keyboardist. The taller one, on lead vocals, sang without an accent and had a sculpted Janet Jackson stomach. Her hair was silky and long. Her Levi's were stonewashed a perfect, off-blue shade.

She wasn't a lounge singer. She looked sexy, comfortable. And the audience *danced*. They *sang along*. "We should learn that one," Karla kept saying. She saw her reflection in the bar mirror and hated her neat peach dress.

She'd been hip once, hadn't she? She'd worn miniskirts with thick belts. There were pictures from the ship, from days off in Barcelona and Nice. That little yellow sundress she used to have. ("Yes," she said to Jack. "I'll have another. It's weird, I don't feel them at all.") They'd rented motorcycles in Saint Lucia and Curaçao and skinny-dipped in Barbados. They'd kissed and kissed in the middle of a restaurant in Margarita.

The band took a break and Jack strode to the stage and Karla played with her straw. He gave Janet Jackson a JOE card. When he returned, Karla said, "I want to be in a band. I feel like I'm forty-five," and Jack seemed to understand and moved his barstool closer to hers.

And then they were back in their own hotel lobby—so white, so shiny—where Karla decided she could step only inside the lines of the tiles. It took quite a while to cross the lobby this way, and that was when Jack told her, "You're drunk."

Karla felt it then, completely.

In the room she said, "Take advantage of me!" and although it was incredibly witty at the time, she'd forget she'd said it. Jack wouldn't remind her.

In the morning, Karla used the whole bottle of shampoo-conditioner and left nothing for Jack. She smelled like very strong limes.

At breakfast they saw the Goodmans, who said nothing about being stood up. Mrs. Goodman plopped down beside Karla and continued her story. She was a math teacher. She'd married Mr. Goodman at twenty, when he was twenty-four. Forty years later, they had four children, and eight grandkids. They'd been to Australia four times. They'd lived in Nice for eight years.

Multiples of four, thought Karla. *Four of us here eating brunch together. Almost four years with Jack and I am almost twenty-six. Which doesn't fit.*

Mr. Goodman shuffled over from the buffet line. "Seven years in Nice, actually," he said.

"You only live once," Mrs. Goodman concluded, and then it seemed to be Karla's turn to speak.

"Jack and I have been lovers for nearly four years," she said.

Jack looked at her.

She didn't know why she'd said it. It certainly wasn't accurate.

Mrs. Goodman nodded. *Lovers—of course!* And she began to ask questions: future plans, how they met, where they wanted to settle, their ages, qualifications, and degrees. Karla decided to say the honest thing, which was she'd like to get into art—photography, maybe, and the Goodmans were quiet for a moment, and Jack looked at her as though she'd turned into a gerbil.

Mr. Goodman looked at his watch. They wanted to attend a Buddhist service. They needed to practice their Mandarin.

Mrs. Goodman pinched him on the arm and said, "The temple will wait," and threatened to give him a Rio de Janeiro, which, she explained, was their synonym for *bruise*, and she began to tell a complicated story involving a Brazilian bicyclist and Mr. Goodman's inability to drink rum. They laughed about their sordid past together.

"Imagine," said Mrs. Goodman. "Forty years I've lived with this man."

Jack got up then, and the good-byes didn't take long, and they were soon back in their pristine room.

A badness was sinking down or rising up, Karla couldn't tell which.

Mrs. Goodman had been *looking* at her. And then Karla hadn't been able to explain properly. Why wasn't she able to explain? "Get into art?" Why was she so bad at talking?

There was something important in this, Karla felt. She only had to go over it again and again to see what it was.

"She had him on a short leash," Jack said. He was rolling up his dirty boxers and putting them in a small plastic bag.

Good for her, thought Karla. She shouldn't speak. Her tone would be all wrong—pointless vitriol. And he would hear it and say something nasty back and begin to hate her.

Jack finished packing his boy things—the leather toiletries bag and the shaving cream that wouldn't fit inside. A book by John Grisham. A red plastic tub of Brylcreem.

Karla gathered things, too, things to take: matches, stationery, unwrapped soap. She was moving without thinking. Her mind was whirling and her body had to keep up. She packed a hotel towel and then put it back. She sniffed a strand of her hair—*yes, limes.*

Why don't we love each other anymore?

"The Goodmans," she began. She wanted to speak before he could, before he asked, *Why did you say "lovers"?* "They just—made me feel bad."

He zipped his leather duffel and looked at her. His forehead was a straight, solid line. His eyes were very green.

"The Goodmans," he said, "are just waiting to die."

Relief swept through. She laughed. Of course! *Waiting to die.* The good, sweet Goodmans. How cruel of him to say and what a kind diversion. How lovely not to be blamed.

NINE

Frank Sinatra

WILLOW FLOATED like a hostess, taking tiny sips of champagne and waiting for 2:00 A.M., when she'd be allowed to have a cigarette. There was no one else left in the bar but Sam and Jack and Karla and Cash from Denver, but these were the Sky Bar rules.

Willow looked at her tiny gold wristwatch.

"No smoke!" said Jack, and waved the pack close to her nose. He slid one out and placed it on the bar.

Cash had arrived at the Palace a month ago and showed no sign of leaving. Karla couldn't remember exactly what he did for a living or why he needed to spend a full month in Shanghai, but tonight he was celebrating. He'd paid for the champagne and poured glasses for all. Willow called him Pang, which meant "fat," which he was. He had a goatee and a kind, red face.

"Smoke," Willow said, and she did, at exactly two o'clock. She turned to Karla and exhaled. "Mr. Marcello. He don't like."

"He doesn't like it when you smoke," said Karla, who had an orchid in her hair.

"No smoke," said Willow, smoking.

Mr. Marcello had come to the Sky Bar at last, several days ago, dressed in a tailored, navy blue suit. He was lean and unassuming, with a plump Paul McCartney bowl cut. "*He's* up-to-date," Jack said between songs, and cued "Let It Be."

"No Mr. Marcello tonight," said Karla. "So you can smoke."

Cash ordered more champagne, and then whiskey and gingers, and before long he and Jack were slurring. Cash's voice boomed, and Sam jumped a little when he spoke. Willow tickled their faces—Jack's, Cash's, Karla's—with a snapped palm frond.

"Good night," Jack announced, back in the room. Karla thought he was saying good night, but he meant the night had been good. At 3:35 A.M. the phone rang and Karla picked it up and heard giggling and a click and Jack knew and smiled and the last thing he said before passing out was her name.

KARLA WENT TO the Italian Exhibition with Willow. "Konsu Italia," it was called. Willow wore a pale pink sundress, sheer and short, and her precious Mr. Marcello shoes. It was very hot, sticky hot, and they walked there from the Palace and then had to wait outside for her friend Jim, the Palace doorman, who didn't show. They ate Popsicles as they waited, which was Willow's idea, and she sucked delicately, without dripping on her dress.

When Willow was done, she took Karla's hand and they charged inside. It was a national holiday, Chinese Labor Day, and the exhibition hall was packed. Everyone pushed.

"Konsu *Italia* and no *Italian* people," said Willow. "Only *Shanghai* people!" They filed past the Tasty Italian Food booths; no sign of Mr. Marcello and his restaurant chain.

They looked at Italian cars, clothes, handbags, wine (free samples), olive oil (no free samples), pianos, sofas, coatracks, doorknobs, and cosmetics, where Willow managed to grab trial lipsticks. There was an entire corridor of "bathroom ware"—bathtubs and sinks, sleek and futuristic, although sticky with fingerprints by now. Willow laughed at the toilet seats: blood red, neon yellow.

"I don't like," she said.

"*I* don't like," Karla agreed.

"*Buon giorno,*" said Willow. "It's *hot!*"

"It's hot."

In the hall center, the Special Italian Acrobatic Team did their hourly show. The routine involved two large girls in tight G-string leotards who curled and wrapped around each other and looked embarrassed and sweaty. Their faces were projected on video screens on either side of the stage. No one clapped.

"Like Sky Bar!" said Willow.

"The outfits?"

"Outfits?"

"No, I know. You mean no clapping," said Karla.

"Yes. No clapping."

They sat down to sample Italian wine at a little table with an umbrella. Willow said, "I like Italian."

They drank, and Willow was tired after the wine. "No sleep," she said. "No sleep last night." She didn't say why.

On the way out, they passed through the Food Court again, and then walked along Zhong Lu, back toward the

Palace Hotel. Willow took Karla's hand again, despite the heat, and said, "Why everyone look at us? They don't see Shanghai person and foreign person together?"

"I guess not." *They stare because you're beautiful. They'll always stare at you.*

"I don't like," said Willow, and squeezed Karla's sweaty hand.

Then they picked up Karla's film, and Karla gave Willow a picture of Jack in front of the Laughing Buddha in Hangzhou because Willow said, "I like," and "Jack is crazy boy!"

Then she kissed Karla good-bye.

"I had a lovely day," said Karla. "Thank you." Willow shrugged and turned to catch her bus back to Pudong.

✧

A "BOTTLE CHUCKER" arrived, and as he juggled glasses and fire, à la *Cocktail,* Karla could have sung *"Titanic"* five times in a row and no one would have noticed. His name was Marty and he was from L.A. He'd been to twenty-one countries and had a Rolodex of five-star hotels—Jack was going to get copies. His own card said, "Martin Sloan, Flair Bartender," and featured a hologram of an exploding martini glass.

He'd done cruise ships, he said, but never R and H.

After work they took Marty to Heaven, where he told them his girlfriend could swallow a knife; she was teaching him how to do it, too. He winked at Jack when he said this, and Karla almost said, "Oh, so I suppose she gives incredible head." But she didn't.

Marty would be there for three weeks, he said. He was really going to miss her—his girlfriend—and her sword-swallowing mouth.

"You'll like Shanghai," said Karla, in a perfectly normal tone. *There are hostess bars on every corner.* "There's so much to see." Jack looked at her, carefully.

She excused herself and spent too long in the bathroom, breathing, willing herself not to scream or cry.

THE NEXT NIGHT was quiet in the bar. Flair wrote them a napkin note: "Can you pick up the pace a bit?"

"Cheeky bastard," said Jack, and acted out "Lyin' Eyes" with hand gestures. Karla laughed, and then they both missed their cues for the next verse. Jack announced, "Sorry. We lost it there for a moment." But no one was listening.

KARLA BEGAN to see shadows of faces from the stage. The bar was so dark and every lyric was so tediously familiar and the candlelight made things wobble and shift sometimes. She'd seen her grandfather and Lady Di and the DJ she'd kissed on the ship.

TOGETHER, in bed, the laptop perched on Jack's belly, they looked things up on Jack's new encyclopedia CD-ROM: Shanghai. Buddhism. Maine. Yorkshire. Hermaphrodites. Bingo. Soccer. Sinatra. Beer.

And when he was gone playing squash the next afternoon: Clitoris. Abstinence. Monogamy. Alcoholism. *Little Women.* All there.

✧

IN JUNE Frank Sinatra died and Newcastle lost to Arsenal in the FA Cup Final. Jack was in mourning.

They took a boat ride along the Huangpu River, at last.

The boat was a small ferry called the *Cupid Feather*, and for seventy yuan they received two B-deck special-class tickets, a cardboard tray with hot tea and stale orange-flavored cookies, and souvenir *Cupid Feather* nail clippers, which Karla would keep in her toiletries bag for years. The ferry pushed away from the Bund, and Karla and Jack watched the streetlamps and the lights strung between, tiny Christmas bulbs, twinkling. There were lights on the Pudong side, too, and lights on the bridge Karla had crossed in the cab with Willow. And then fewer and fewer lights, only shadows of sleeping cranes and cargo containers. Their own boat was quiet and eel-like, slipping cleanly through black water.

Most of the passengers stayed inside drinking beer, but Karla and Jack were at the bow, close but not touching. Karla thought of the crew deck behind the Maria Lounge, that looking-over-the-rail feeling. She told Jack and he said he remembered it, too, and for several seconds they were back there together, new to each other, new to all those pretty cities and islands. She remembered the smells of coal and stale cigarette smoke covered up with citrus. The old matted carpets, fluffed and vacuumed daily. The rhinestone necklace she'd lost in the life-jacket closet, her evening dress hiked up to her waist, thick coiled rope against the backs of her thighs. Rope to rescue people. Life-jackets like pillows, absorbing their sounds and smells.

And then they were back at the Bund.

"Short trip," said Jack.

Karla asked if she could have his nail clippers, and he said yes.

"That was fun," Karla announced in the cab. "The lights were pretty."

"They were," said Jack.

They said nothing else for a while, which made it easier to convince themselves.

They went to Heaven for chicken quesadillas. Karla had one Long Island iced tea, and that was enough. Jack had two. Tammy opened the French doors and placed a few tables on the sidewalk, and there they sat.

"I feel like I'm in Spain," Jack said, probably because the Gipsy Kings were playing. And then a small boy appeared. He pointed into his paper cup and then to his mouth. His hands were black. Jack gave him the basket of popcorn from the table and five one-yuan coins.

We should be having a Life conversation, Karla thought. Maybe in having it they would want to act it out. Something about restoring an old farmhouse in the Lake District or in Maine. The details could remain fuzzy in order to avoid the two largest questions: What would they do for work? and How would they live there legally without being married?

"That boy," said Karla. "Did you see his hands?"

"We're very lucky," he said. "We weren't born here."

It would make so much sense to stick together after all this time, after so many contracts invested.

"We're lucky," Karla repeated.

IN THE MORNING they watched a John Candy film in bed and laughed—bad breath, boozy, sweaty pores, comforting hotel sheets. They descended just in time for brunch, wrinkled and bleary. They squinted in the sunny atrium, where guests with cigars and sunglasses drank very small cups of coffee. Jack drank Karla's mimosa.

"No squash today," he said.

"Fuck squash," said Karla.

He looked at her, surprised. "Why fuck squash?"

"It's just an expression."

"Why shouldn't I play squash?"

"I didn't say that. It's just nice to have a different day. Away from the computer. Away from squash."

"I like squash."

"I know you like squash. I was just saying, it's nice to spend time together."

His eyebrows went up.

"I mean like this, during the day."

"Maybe I'd feel better after a game."

"After your mimosa?"

"Christ, it's brunch."

"There's nothing wrong with drinking a mimosa."

"I'm going up," he said, and patted his pocket for his room card key. "Sign the check?"

"Why are you running away from me?"

"I've changed my mind. I'm playing squash. Fucking squash."

"Fuck squash. I said 'Fuck squash.' And now you're mad because I said it? Am I not supposed to say things?"

He took a long swallow, finishing the mimosa. "I'm not speaking like this, not in front of everybody. Whoops!" He did a mock drunk stumble. "Too pissed to play squash." He turned and left.

She thought it all through, back and forth and over and over, until her omelet began to congeal.

"More coffee, Miss Kala?"

"No thanks," she said, and smiled for the waiter, falsely.

"You look tired today, I think," he said.

She nodded, and he moved to the next table.

She was tired. She felt it in her gut.

SHE FOUND HIM in the room, staring at the computer screen.

"Did we really have an argument about squash?" she said.

"We're both cranky," he explained, and switched gears, as she knew he would. He decided to talk shop—JOE. He'd received a fax from a hotel in Bangkok. They needed a four-piece.

Karla wasn't playing. "Why do you think we fight like that, pick at each other like that?"

"Why are you pushing this?" His eyes were clear and green. Why did booze do that to him, make him prettier?

"We don't fuck anymore," she said. She'd said it.

"I know," he said. He chose not to comment on her word choice, not immediately. He said nothing for a very long time and then, unable to resist, "Nice language."

"We don't," she said.

"I know," he said. "You made your point." His back was to her now. Big, still back. Shoulders hunched. Pale blue polo shirt. She imagined hugging him from behind, nuzzling his neck. She couldn't bring herself to do it.

"We have to talk about it," she said. "Figure out why."

"I'm not up for that right now," he said. His voice was even. He stared at his screen.

In the gym, Karla undressed and spent a solid hour in the sauna, memorizing her new Magic Trax songs, "Never Ever" by All Saints and "You Needed Me" by Anne Murray. So many wimpy girl lyrics.

THEY GOT A LETTER at last from Milk and Honey, all the way from Muscat, and Jack decided he missed the Gulf. He wanted to set up an all-expenses paid JOE trip. He began to make phone calls and send faxes. He made bad jokes about camels.

"We could spend a week in Dubai, after we're done. And then we could crash with Milk and Honey for a night or two."

Karla didn't want to crash with Milk and Honey, but she went along with it. Just to pretend to agree on something. It was a nice idea, that elsewhere they might be different. That China was the problem.

They just couldn't talk about it, and still work together every night. And so they didn't.

"MAYBE I COULD go back to school," said Karla. It was morning and Jack was positioned at the desk, about to pack up for the Business Center. Karla sipped her instant coffee in bed. "Art school, maybe. I don't know. I need to research, find out if I could do it part-time."

Jack looked up. "In America?"

"Or England—wherever. I'd have to get in first. I need to research. Online. Or maybe a library? I don't know."

His eyes were locked on his mini-stapler. "Go for it," he said, not unkindly, but as though he'd reluctantly given permission.

THE SHANGHAI Library had a big English section, Karla discovered, and it was only twenty minutes from the Palace by foot. She found a coffee-stained *Guide to U.S. Graduate Degrees,* three years old, but art schools were listed. She had a notebook and a Palace pen. She filled two pages.

KARLA DRANK coconut milk through a straw from a thick, aluminum can as she walked back, and the drink seemed to restore something in her, seemed to ease a tightness. Drizzle landed on her bare arms, and this too felt nice. She passed a market stall where a stooped woman (white nightdress in the middle of the day) wrapped rubber bands around hand-size bundles of scallions. Tiny bench on the pavement, tiny bundles accumulating beside her.

The drizzle became heavier, and poncho-wearing bicy-clists filed past, their hands and arms hidden under cloaks of plastic—blue, red, purple, yellow, green—screaming to be photographed, and this time Karla could watch as long as she wanted. The traffic cop dropped his hand, and a throng of colors and wheels charged by. *I am witnessing a great treat.* She was part of it somehow. She was *experiencing China.*

She passed the hospital, where a man with a bloody fore-head was being led by the arm to the emergency entrance.

She saw a woman massaging her feet with an abacus and a man selling bear claws, antlers, and small, stuffed porcu-pines from a square of yellow cloth.

At the hotel, the airport bus waited for travelers to board. She knew that feeling, the thrill of waving good-bye, of setting oneself in motion. The real fun was in coming and going, not staying.

And yet, today: a city walk to the library. Negotiating this place a little, having a haunt or two. Knowing her way there and back. She could do this anywhere if she could do it in Shanghai.

MARGARET, behind the Sky Bar bar, mixed a cosmopolitan and told Karla she should eat more. Then she asked if Karla and Jack wanted to go dancing at a German brewpub called Steiney's.

"Too tired," said Karla. The last time they'd gone out with Margaret, she'd ordered rounds for strangers and left them with the tab.

Instead, after work, they played Karaoke, which meant they all took turns on the mike and Jack played the songs and Karla hit the tambourine and sang harmonies. Karla wasn't in the mood for any of this after four sets, but Jack was. He was thrilled. The free drinks flowed.

Willow did "My Heart Will Go On," with breathy determination ("Neee, faaaaaa, wheh-EEEH-vah yoo aww…"). Sam and Margaret did an impassioned rendition of "Unbreak My Heart," but it was in the wrong key for both and Jack was too drunk to transpose on his acoustic. Willow said "Un-break My Heart" was a girls' song, and Sam blushed but kept singing. Then Cash had a go with "House of the Rising Sun" and was badly out of tune, and still Jack was smiling. Jack was good at this, humoring people without letting them know. Karla was not good at it. People could see when she was fibbing.

"You're a bad liar," Karla's mother had said once. Her mother meant the orange Popsicle left on top of the washing machine and the reply "It wasn't me." And the afternoon Karla was supposed to be at Drama Club when really she was letting Drew Becker touch her breasts in the Beckers' guest bedroom.

Jack was a good liar. In Dubai, he'd once told Karla he was staying in the bar to have a nightcap. Karla left him there and crossed the lobby to their ground-floor room. She read and brushed and flossed and enjoyed the time by herself. She slept soundly.

She woke in a panic at 4:00 A.M., when headlights from

the street shone in. She looked out and there was Jack, getting out of a taxi.

Karla waited and reviewed her options: Say something or not. The door clicked open as quietly as possible.

"I saw you," she said instantly. "You just got out of a cab."

"What were you doing, spying on me?"

So damn quick. She had to admire him for it.

"I went for a falafel. I didn't feel like walking back."

A lie, Karla knew, but a reasonable one. She had to drop it, or risk being called paranoid, or risk revealing her own se-crets. The Boston numbers on the York phone bill, for starters. "My old roommate," she'd said, which was partly true. If Jack had ever suspected it was Arthur, the long-abandoned Boston boyfriend, he'd never said so.

And so the falafel place it was.

This didn't seem distant, and Karla was angry again, re-membering. The Gotham Bar fibs could now be added to his list.

Jack was strumming for Cash and pretending Cash was a fabulous singer, and Willow was smoking and Margaret was washing the last of the glasses and soon they would all be gone and Karla and Jack, in their little room, would watch TV and Karla would read and then they would both sleep without speaking about any of the important things.

How long can a person do this, without imploding, with-out beginning to hate herself? What happens when the im-plosion finally comes?

✦

THEY HAD THREE months left. Karla decided to take Man-darin lessons.

On the Bund the week before, Karla's tutor, Beth, had probably noticed Karla's camera and notebook and ponytailed hair.

"Excuse me, but would you like to learn Mandarin?" Beth asked.

In the space of an hour, ten Chinese students had already asked Karla to "Practice English, please."

"Yes. Maybe," said Karla, surprising herself. Beth was an English major at Fudan University. She carried a heavy backpack and wore a faint smudge of purple lip gloss. Her white winter coat was worn but clean. Karla took her number.

"My name is from the very famous *Little Women*," added Beth, before they parted ways.

When Karla told Jack, he asked, "Is she expensive? Does she have a sister?"

"I want to speak to people here," Karla said.

BETH ARRIVED promptly at 11:00 A.M. in the Palace lobby.

"I saw it on TV," Karla said, after shaking Beth's hot, damp hand. "*Little Women*, with Winona Ryder."

Beth was impressed. "Of course," she said. "The movie. I have heard about it." She'd never heard of Winona Ryder.

They stood in the Palace lobby and Beth gaped at the marble, the brass elevators. She seemed shorter today. She wore a pale yellow sweatshirt with small birds painted on the sleeves. By the time they reached Karla's floor, she'd invited Karla to her house to try her mother's dumplings.

"That would be wonderful," said Karla, and pushed her key card through the slot. She hoped Jack had put on pants, and he had (shorts). He was going to the gym, which Karla had suggested. Beth blushed deeply and shook his hand.

"Don't drink all the beer in the fridge, you two," he said.

"You, too," said Beth.

She turned to look out the window, cheeks flushed, and Karla offered Lipton tea.

BETH HAD borrowed her niece's old grammar book, which had pencil doodles throughout. Her niece was now eight, and the pictures were cartoonlike and faded, but Karla could understand them, with Beth's explanations. She asked Beth to recite numbers and greetings into a tape recorder. Beth did this slowly, and giggled. She'd never recorded her voice before.

"I want to be a journalist," Beth said. "To tape the voices and interpret and write the events."

"This is good practice," said Karla.

Beth said she wanted to read as many books in English as possible. Karla agreed to make a list of her favorites, for next time. Then she paid Beth fifty yuan. Beth seemed to feel bad about this, but took it.

"You will be a very bright student," Beth promised.

THE NEXT WEEK Karla met Beth at the gate of the Botanical Gardens. Beth checked the meter of Karla's cab to make sure she hadn't been overcharged.

"We'll stroll later," Beth said, "but first, dumplings," which her mother had been preparing all morning just a few blocks away.

Beth's mother wore tiny pearl earrings and a faded green apron and a stern, weary expression. Karla said hello and how are you, exhausting her Mandarin, and replaced her shoes with slippers.

Beth had her own room, with bright wooden floors and

new furniture and a little balcony looking out over gray buildings. She showed Karla her parents' room, which was bigger. Both rooms had large TVs.

A tray of sliced honeydew melon had been left for them, and a bowl of strawberries. Mom perched on Beth's bed and said, "I hope now Beth can come visit you in America."

Beth translated and Karla nodded. It seemed sudden, the trade-off. "I'll feed her lobster there. As much as she can possibly eat."

Mom smiled and went to get the dumplings, a special recipe from one of the northern provinces, and Karla and Beth ate from a communal bowl, dropping each dumpling into a smaller bowl of spicy soy. "It slithers, I think," said Beth, who left her dumpling in the sauce for a full minute before eating it.

"Yes, slithers."

"Have you had this before?"

"No," Karla lied. "My first time." Willow's frozen dumplings had been smaller, starchier. It was cold at Beth's, too, and Karla was full quickly, and there was nothing to wash it all down with. Beth's mother, meanwhile, was filling the dumpling bowl again. She brought in a tiny wooden stool and told Karla to sit down and lean over and get her face in close, as Beth did.

"What are you doing in Shanghai?" Mom asked. Beth paused to translate, and kept her eyes fixed on the dumplings.

She must have known already, but Karla told her. "I'm a singer at the Palace."

"Part-time or professional?" Mom asked.

"Professional. I work six days per week."

Mom nodded curtly and left the room again.

Beth put down her chopsticks to show Karla her tapes, called "Crazy English," which were collected TV broadcasts and movie excerpts and interviews with celebrities. She played one that announced the death of Princess Diana, complete with "Candle in the Wind" and Blair's funeral speech. She had tapes called "Music Treats" with random Top 40 songs. And, of course, she had a bootleg copy of the *Titanic* soundtrack.

Then Beth took a picture (Karla, hunched over the dumpling bowl), and that was absolutely the last one Karla could manage to swallow.

"My mother," Beth explained, "will now prepare a supper." They would all eat together when Beth's father returned from work.

I'm going to vomit, Karla thought.

"We should begin walking," Beth suggested. "Good for the digestion." They cleared their plates and put on their shoes quickly and bypassed Beth's mother, who was watching TV in her bedroom.

On the street boys smashed red berries against the pavement and girls played a game with elastic bands tied together to make a jump rope. Each girl had to jump over the bands quickly or risk getting tangled.

"Good jumpers are rewarded with status in school," Beth explained. "If a girl is good at this game, I think she will be very popular. I am too old for this game. And I am not a good jumper." But she bounced along, humming, talking, swinging her arms. She slowed her pace a little for Karla.

"The lazy life!" she said, and Karla didn't know if she meant the weekend or Karla's pace of walking or Karla's whole life in general.

So Karla said, "I'm just waking up," by way of explanation. She felt a headache creeping in, in fact, and wished she'd brought her sunglasses. The day was becoming warm and bright, if not clear.

They reached the Botanical Gardens, and Karla tried to be perkier. Inside there were palm trees and rose beds and little lakes and bridges, all well-manicured. They kept talking as they strolled, about Beth's classes and where Karla and Jack had been. Beth wanted to know about Abu Dhabi because it was somewhat like Egypt and it was her dream to go to Egypt. She had a map in her room, which she'd shown Karla, kneeling on the hard floor to point to Cairo. She wanted to see a real camel, not one from the Shanghai Zoo.

Then it was Karla's turn to ask. She referred to her mental list:

1. Why were the temples yellow?
2. Why were the coats blue?
3. What did Beth's father do? (How could they afford two TVs?)
4. Why was Beth allowed to have siblings when Willow was not?
5. Cultural Revolution—Thoughts? Comments?
6. Cruise ships—Why don't they come to Shanghai?

Beth answered as thoroughly as she could:

1. I don't know. Because Buddha is always the yellow color. Gold.
2. Oh yes, this is a Mao thing. To make a unified China with the heart, all Chinese people together and strong. But only the old people are wearing this coat now.

3. He's an engineer. He designed airplanes, long ago, and now he's designing washing machines. He knows some English, so you can talk to him later.

4. Yes, I have—siblings? Siblings. A sister who will be a teacher and a brother who works in a bank already. This is a tricky thing. At first Mao tells all the Chinese to pro-create, and for a time it is normal to have big families—six, seven, eight. But this is different today. There are new government rules: only one child. But the rule is some-times...flex.

"Flexible."

The rule is sometimes flex-ible. If the two only chil-dren marry each other, they can have the two. And some in the country still have many kids for free work. Free labor. And they don't get caught. And sometimes if they have too many girls and want a boy, they keep trying and nobody cares. And some, like my parents, just don't fol-low and no one complains. So it is a rule but not a hard one, I think.

5. Mother and Father were sent away to the country when they were young, and when they came back they had the blisters on the hands. They say, "This is good, to feel the hands and know the person has experienced this." But I don't have to go to the country, and that is better.

6. Hong Kong has the cruise ships because the shopping is better there.

They passed the bonsai tree display, and Karla thought of *The Karate Kid*. "It's pretty," she said.

"But cruel," said Beth, because the roots and branches had to be twisted, forced.

"Like the feet of Chinese women, long ago," Karla said, and imagined Jack's reaction.

Beth said yes, she knew exactly what Karla meant. Her friend's grandmother had had this done. She folded her fingers under to show Karla what happened to the toes.

"And they couldn't walk, but men think this is very beautiful."

Karla said, "Like high heels." Beth nodded, but they both knew it was nothing like high heels. "I have to wear high heels for my job," Karla said. She couldn't seem to stop herself. "Every night. I like sneakers better."

"But you can't wear sneakers with skirts," said Beth.

"No, you can't," said Karla. It was amazing how much Beth understood.

They looked at large, carved stones mounted on wooden platforms. "This is the ancient way of art, to be free," Beth explained.

Karla scrolled back, Intro to Art History. The word *Doric* floated up, and she pushed it back down.

They wandered past a little amusement park—go-carts, bumper cars, shooting targets for prizes—and Karla hoped Beth didn't want to do these things. She led Karla instead to a large metal bowl with copper handles, filled with water. They paid one yuan each and rubbed the handles very hard and fast with wet palms, and electric ripples appeared on the water's surface. "It's a kind of old Chinese magic, a phenomenon," said Beth.

Phenomenon. Was she showing off? It took Karla a while to rub the right way, but she got it eventually. "Neat," she said, and they wandered off again.

They passed a lake with a statue in the middle: a small girl and boy clinging to the side of a large, scaly fish. This meant happiness and wealth, said Beth. "Prosperity."

Everything stood for something else—all this common knowledge shared by a billion people, and Karla was oblivious.

Karla thought of the Lake District, because of all the green, she supposed, and she began to describe the camping trip she and Jack had taken there. She mentioned Wordsworth and Keats, and Beth didn't know who they were.

Karla felt a little triumphant, and then a little guilty.

"I think I need glasses," she said, to make them even again.

"I also do," said Beth. She had to sit at the very front of the class to see, she said.

Karla's headache was in full bloom. She wanted a beer. "Gum?" She dug in her purse and found some.

"Oh yes," said Beth.

"My mother hates to see me chew gum," said Karla. "She says it makes me look like a cow."

Beth smiled. "My mother hates when I—" She snapped her fingers.

"Snap."

"Snap. It reminds her of a rascal."

Karla snapped nightly, like a banshee, like a rascal, during almost every song. It was her tic, she knew.

And then Beth asked about Abu Dhabi again, and Karla described it all in more detail: the city buildings, the desert, the camels, the mosques, the white robes, and the veiled women walking ten paces behind. Beth listened intently, and Karla enjoyed speaking at length. She realized just how rarely she did it.

"Do you want to see the market?" Beth asked, and so they

left the park and crossed the street. The merchandise was familiar: Spice Girls posters and slippers and belts and hair clips, then eggs and rice and burlap sacks of loose tea and cucumbers and strange squashes and bunches of carrots and leafy things. Men sold the knickknacks and women sold the vegetables. The women had weathered hands and faces dark from the sun. Their shoes were muddy.

"From the country," said Beth, leading Karla through. "They come by bicycle. They come early in the morning. At that time the price is more expensive. In the afternoon it's cheaper."

There were bright red buckets, and a complicated network of hoses, and tubs of live eels, frogs, and turtles. Everything seemed to be moving, jumping, scrambling. The net above the frog bucket jerked up in places, little pockets of frog popcorn popping. The eel creatures were not eels but snakes, coiled and spinning so slowly Karla's toes clenched. A man in blue grabbed the top coil and skinned it alive, right in front of them, the dark outside sliced with a blade and peeled from the white snake flesh underneath, flesh that still wriggled, a blue organ of some kind dangling. Even Beth gaped a little.

"I'm sorry!" she said, and led Karla away. Karla's hands were in fists; she was scared of touching something by mistake. "Don't look down," said Beth. Karla looked. There were small piles of entrails by the sidewalk, little looped intestines and brains. There was blood. Something was happening to Karla at last, something bodily. Her own organs were churning.

She didn't want Beth to think she was crazy. "I'm squeamish," she said. *I was a vegetarian once.* (What was Beth's mother making for dinner?) *My boyfriend is not really my boyfriend anymore.*

"I don't eat the frogs," Beth said quickly. "But snake is okay. We say that inside each animal is hot or cold. Snake is cold. And hot or cold helps with the balance inside."

"Yes, I've heard this," Karla answered. "Like yin and yang."

"Not exactly," said Beth. "But that is also important, yin and yang." She seemed pleased that Karla knew these words at least.

"I'm sorry," Karla said. "I like the markets."

"But you are squeamish." This was a new word for Beth, and she said it to herself several more times before they arrived home.

Karla was given the best chair, with a pink cushion, and the biggest glass of Coke. Beth's father said, "Pleased to make your acquaintance," and found it hard to meet Karla's eyes. They sat at a card table, slurping over bowls again, taking from communal pots of lovely, harmless vegetables, mostly. There were green beans and pickled cucumber and a tomato soup they called Russian with pork and cabbage, and cold duck, which was lean and sweet, and small fish, fried whole, mouths gaping open. This was the only thing Karla didn't want to eat, but Beth's mom pointed and nodded, and Karla had no choice. She nibbled at a scale or two and said, "Mmm," and that seemed to suffice. Mom belched loudly, three or four times, and Karla knew Jack would have burped right back at her.

She wanted Jack to be there. He would've made them laugh. He would've finished his share of dumplings.

Karla offered to help clear, but they wouldn't let her, and instead Beth's father began to wash the dishes.

Beth rubbed her belly and said, "A good cook will hold

on to her husband tightly." She giggled. "My mother says this. But I can't cook."

"Neither can I," said Karla.

Beth's mother asked where Karla's boyfriend was. "Not feeling well," Karla said, and Mom said he must come next time and Karla promised that he would.

"I should go soon," Karla blurted, unable to think of a better way. "I have to get ready for work." Beth translated, and after good-byes and handshakes and many *sheh sheh*s and more pictures, which Karla promised to copy, Beth escorted Karla to the street and hailed a cab.

Karla managed to say "Palace Hotel" in the magic roller-coaster way—three tones, up, down, down further. Once Karla had ended up at Yangzi Suites, Flynn and Glo territory, and had prayed neither had seen her. But the taxi was heading the right way, past the museum and the shopping plaza and the old temple.

In the cab, Karla could at last stop grinning inanely. Her mouth was greasy and spicy, and she wanted to drink many tall glasses of water to wash the fish taste away.

She practiced her version of events for Jack. There was something very specific about the snake she'd wanted to describe, something both scary and exciting—but it was gone.

✧

TO MIX IT UP a little, Jack and Karla decided to go out before work, to see Velocity's first set at the Hard Rock Cafe. Norm the guitarist put their drinks on his tab and then hurried off to the soundboard to adjust something. He still wore his leather vest. He smiled at Karla from stage.

"They're good," Jack said.

The girl singer wasn't fabulous but she was into it. She wore a tight tube top thing with zippers, and even when she wasn't singing, she was swaying in a convincing way. *Of course*, thought Karla. *Swaying.*

She tried it that night, during "Three Times a Lady."

"Stop," said Jack. "You're making me seasick."

After work—they were on a roll—they went to Steiney's, the German club, where, on three crowded floors, Chinese people drank German beer and danced to a Filipino duo. Jack and Karla said little and watched the duo and dancers from the highest story.

Karla still had her camera in her bag. She slid it out carefully and shot a quick picture of Jack, looking over the railing. He didn't notice until the flash went off.

Later they would both be surprised at how sad he looked in the picture, how quiet.

"And I wasn't even pissed," he would say.

"Why did you take my picture?" he asked, as she put her camera away in Steiney's.

"You look thoughtful. I like candids," she said.

It makes you look at me.

TEN

Gloria Gaynor

JACK WAS PLEASED with his latest purchase, a tiny blue and silver desk lamp with a very bright bulb.

"But we're leaving in two months," Karla said. *Why bother?*

"We're here now," he said. "And I can't see."

KARLA ASKED Margaret to define *"ma ma hoo hoo."* She'd forgotten to ask Beth. "I hear it all the time."

"So-so," said Margaret, shaking a martini. "Not good and not bad. Just okay. The real meaning is 'horse horse, tiger tiger.'"

"Comme ci, comme ça."

"Oui," said Margaret.

She invited Karla to an aerobics class at the Body Lady Club, and Karla accepted.

It was good for Karla to sweat in spandex again and satisfying to use her dance head in a small way. Easy step, pivot step, grapevine—a Rodgers and Hammerstein Review staple on the ship. She knew this stuff. She was a Singer Who Moves Well.

There were twenty other women in the class, all Chinese. There was no AC. During the fifth set of power squats, Karla began to feel a little faint. She knew her face was very red. Margaret, barely sweating at all, was kind enough not to comment. She wore a white sports bra, her nipples blaring through. How did she get to the point of not caring?

And then Karla fell. When she came to, Margaret and her sports bra were looming overhead.

"How you feeling?" she asked.

"*Ma ma hoo hoo,*" said Karla. She sat the sixth set out.

✧

THEY SANG FOR A Chinese wedding in the hotel's Pretty Petal Reception Room. The bride wanted "I Will Always Love You" as she walked down the aisle, and Karla was nervous about the high notes. She had to have a glass of champagne beforehand and still the "you—oooo-ooo" parts were wobbly and thin, like a child singing, like a pathetic little girl. She smiled harder—*It doesn't matter, it doesn't matter*—and Jack did the same.

"A hundred bucks richer for twenty minutes of work," he said when it was done. The photographer, a wiry Chinese man with a shock of white hair, was setting up in front of them. He fiddled with his tripod and didn't look at them and didn't say, "Nice job," or "Sounds great," or even, "Whitney!"

"A hundred bucks," Jack said again. He meant, *"Forget about it."*

But it mattered to Karla. A squeaky stupid song. It made her want to hide somewhere in Maine and take up knitting and wear overalls and not wash her hair. She kept failing at this, her job.

She understood Sid the Comedian's question then: *"Am I funny?"* He meant, *"Will I always suck or is this just a phase?"*

If she asked out loud (*"Am I any good?"*), Jack wouldn't answer, just as Karla hadn't answered Sid. There was no right answer except yes. And if the answer was yes, you didn't need to ask.

THEY DID COLORS and animals during Karla's next lesson. She asked Beth if they could do jobs and countries.

"It's in the next book," said Beth, who was becoming less and less impressed with Karla's aptitude for language. "You should practice this one first."

KARLA STIRRED, still fuzzy from an afternoon nap. Crisp hotel sheets, Paul Simon on low, through headphones, the one about the wall in China, so many miles long. Jack tapped at his keyboard in the blue lamp shadow, and a bright beam shone through the curtain gap. He'd given up on the Business Center. He seemed to enjoy typing in his underwear.

Karla had been drifting, the vague impression of a crowded street far below, the pleasure of bed and bra in the afternoon. She'd had the same kinds of drugged naps on the ship, the porthole light shining in (when she'd had a porthole), stealing twenty minutes before dinner, or sleepy on a beach because of afternoon beer—the sweaty, sudden start and the dry mouth when waking. Under the practice room pianos, at college. Thin, rough carpet and the strong smell of feet.

She'd seen Norm from the Hard Rock Cafe, too. In near-sleep he'd finally come to see them in the Sky Bar, without his vest, without any clothes at all.

"You do that one well," he'd said. He meant "My Funny Valentine," which she'd delivered expertly. The bar shimmered with applause. "It's yours. Your song."

Yes, she thought. *I know. And no one has ever noticed.*

"Up?" said Jack.

She pretended not to be.

✧

WILLOW SAT ON a plastic bucket, sobbing, in the back room with the vast tub of peanuts and the dirty glasses.

"What's wrong?" said Karla, who'd come for nuts. Willow said nothing, so Karla squatted beside her, careful not to stretch the hem of her dress. It seemed impolite to grab a handful now.

"My boyfriend," Willow said, at last.

"Mr. Marcello?"

She shook her head. "My boyfriend."

"Mr. Marcello?"

"I don't know."

Was there another one? Jim the doorman?

"Boyfriend. He is now very…angry." She sniffed and waited for Karla to respond.

"Fuck it," Karla said, standing up, having no idea what Willow meant exactly. "*Fuck* him. You know what I mean?"

"Fuck. Him," said Willow, without enthusiasm. She sniffed and wiped her hands on her *qi pao.*

"Yes. Fuck him."

"I know this already. *Fuck. Shit. Motherfucker.*"

"Yes, good words," said Karla. Then Margaret appeared with a tray of empty glasses. Willow sniffed. Karla scooped her hand into the bottomless peanut barrel and began to chew.

"Do you think I'm funny?" Karla tried in Mandarin, when Margaret had left.

"Jack, yes. You, *ma ma hu hu*," said Willow. "But good Chinese, Ka-la." She rose from the bucket and was gone.

✧

KARLA TOOK another class with Margaret, and this time a British woman was there, compact and gray-haired. She stood in the front row and gave little yelps of encouragement when the power squats began. Karla followed her lead and just about did them all.

There were new steps to learn: knee step, side step, thigh step, four step, double step, indecision step. Karla liked the close, industrious limbs. She liked the techno beat and even the yeasty smell of sweat, like the smell in the girls' dressing room before each ship show, the smell of nervous divas.

They changed and deodorized, and Karla asked about Willow.

"Willow's boyfriend is married," said Margaret. "I say to her months ago this no good."

"Oh," said Karla. "You mean Mr. Marcello?"

"I mean the boyfriend. But Marcello is married also, yes," said Margaret. "You want the bubble tea today?"

✧

IT WAS ALOHA WEEK in the Continental Café. A guest chef from Oahu arrived with six hula girls who danced on a stage beside the Continental buffet table, right before Karla and Jack's first set. The dancers had incredible teeth, golden skin. Their hair gleamed; their curves were beautifully symmetrical. For their finale they mouthed the words to "Margaritaville" in Hawaiian as a track blared behind them.

Jack sat facing the stage during dinner, six nights in a row.

In the Sky Bar, at the end of Aloha Week, a Scottish pilot with a Chinese girlfriend asked Karla, "How come you don't wear a grass skirt?"

Jack and the Scot and the girlfriend laughed, and Karla excused herself and in the ladies' room she checked the smile she'd pasted on. It was mostly convincing.

The bathroom attendant offered her a tissue, but Karla refused and locked herself in a stall. The shiny black floors reflected up, and Karla wondered if the attendant could see her there, squatting, or if she liked the muffled sounds of their music playing, the strains of Northern Lights.

The gentlemen's room also had an attendant, Jack confirmed. Jack called him the Tweezer Man, because, like his colleague in the ladies', he picked up each new hand towel with shiny brass tongs.

I should never, ever complain about my job, Karla thought, crouching.

They were past the seven-month mark; one month left to go.

KARLA LEFT HER notebook in the back of a taxi and Jack made two phone calls. Three hours later it was returned.

"Told you," said Jack. "Why don't you have faith?"

The drivers were scared of punishment, Karla imagined. Theft = jail. And very few English scribbles turned up in the lost and found department. But it *was* remarkable, to find it again.

On the first page she'd written, "Portland School of Art, Maine. Low residency." Low residency meant she'd only have to be there twice a year, two weeks each time. In between she'd correspond with a supervisor. She'd be expected to produce a complete portfolio, if she got in.

She could keep working that way. Singing.

What if she did apply? She liked photography. Maybe getting the list of schools back meant she needed them.

"It's an omen," she said. "Maybe it means I'm going to be a famous artist."

"Maybe it means you have a bloody smart boyfriend," Jack said.

It seemed strange to hear him call himself that, her boyfriend. Of course he was.

✧

KARLA SIPPED A ginger ale and felt a hard pinch on her shoulder.

"New shoes!" said Willow.

"Yes, new shoes," said Karla. They admired Karla's dangling feet: fake leather, narrow heel, on sale on Nanjing Lu.

"I like."

Karla waited, but that was all.

✧

KARLA WAS OFF sick. Her throat was scratchy and dry, as though she'd swallowed a tiny piece of plastic wrapper. She hadn't missed one night of work since Abu Dhabi. She'd shown up, coughed off mike, focused on her tambourine.

Now she wondered: What if she lost her voice completely? It might be a relief. She'd be excused.

But she wouldn't lose her voice. The plastic wrapper feeling would pass quickly because the rest of her felt fine. Just a cold. Jack wouldn't have to work on his own for long.

She drank tea in the room. Willow called and said, "I miss you!" and Margaret called to see if she was up for aerobics the next day. "Sorry," said Karla. Sam, at 1:00 A.M., asked if she needed to be escorted to the hospital.

"It's just a cold," she said. "It's just that I can't sing right now."

"Okay," said Sam. "And by the way, Jack would like to stay here for a while, to help me with my small problem."

"Sure," said Karla. "What problem?"

"My drinking problem!" Sam squealed, and hung up.

WHEN HER VOICE came back, two nights later, the songs seemed fresh. She was a little hoarse and she liked the sound. Sexy. Worldly.

"You'll get it back," said Jack.

"I know I'll get it back," she said.

"Just saying," he said.

IN TRUTH, Karla was scared every night, and she was tired of being scared, tired of her own cycle of pathetic thoughts. She couldn't make them stop.

She'd tried, on occasion, to explain this to Jack.

Scared? he'd said. It was a stupid bar. No one was listening.

It wasn't the songs. Within the 3.5 minutes of each track, everything was predetermined, safe. She knew exactly what to do now. She only had to say the words at the right time in the right order and everything would be fine. She swerved carefully from the high notes. She smiled ironically if the lyrics were overly corny. And then the next song would begin and then the next.

But there was no guarantee that the next one would come quickly enough. In between there would be little or no clapping. Jack would fiddle with his effects pedal. He might not speak at all these days. And then they'd all be looking at her because there was too much silence. *What's going on?* they wondered, collectively. *What happened to the music?* They began to hate the ones responsible for the empty, awkward seconds.

Karla fiddled, too. She adjusted her microphone stand, although it was the perfect height. She stared at the song list, willing it to help her. Next to Song Number 413, "You're So Vain," she'd typed "Carey Simon" and every night she noticed and swore she'd print out a corrected copy the next day. Then she drank and forgot, or remembered and felt silly. But maybe it really was the typo's fault. If they had the missing *l*, everything would change, everything would be smooth and easy and the guests would clap or at the very least *not look at her during the silences* and Karla would relax then, and maybe even enjoy it. She would breathe and nail the high notes, and Jack would think, *Wow, she's good,* and say, "Nice job, Kar. That last one—way to go." And she'd say thanks and that night he'd kiss her carefully, appreciatively, when they returned to the room.

But in real life each song ended, and each time Karla had nothing to say. What was wrong with her? The words just didn't come out in a logical way. She'd said once, after wine, "I love this next tune, about a 'Big Old Yellow Taxi'—" and Jack had cut her off.

"You sound blotto," he'd whispered.

She'd wanted to slap him, and instead she had to smile, smile, her bra falling down, a sharp twinge in her lower back. She bent her knees a little to ease it and smiled, smiled. If they could sit down onstage, it would be better. Maybe the words would come quickly then. But Jack thought it looked bad to sit. It looked lazy, he said.

"Gin Fizz sits down," she said.

"And?"

She knew his back hurt, too, the weight of the electric guitar pressing down.

She considered telling the Sky Bar guests the truth: *It's not my fault. I know all my words and Jack doesn't.*

She considered her tambourine. During the first week in Abu Dhabi, she'd had a bruise on her thigh from the banging. She'd since learned to tap lightly. She wished for a bruise now, for distraction.

"It's hard to blame them, you know," Jack had whispered, during a recent silence. "I wouldn't clap for us either."

"BET YOU MISSED ME," Karla said in the Sky Bar, during the break. "Two nights on your own. Must have been hard for you to carry off 'Power of Love.'"

"It wasn't requested," he said. "I played the Male Country Disc, twice. It was fine."

"Like I said, you must have missed me," she said.

"No need to be a smart-ass, Kar. You're back now, so drop it."

"Maybe I'll get sick more often. Maybe I'll start licking doorknobs."

He turned to look for a waitress, to order something, and she made herself stop, at least out loud.

ELEVEN

Eurythmics

KARLA WAS STILL PROUD of their name, Northern Lights. It was an uncommon name for a duo. It was what she and Jack had in common—northern places, Maine and Yorkshire. She'd thought of it in a York café, sipping Earl Grey and reading *The Stage*. It had been one of Jack's Canary weeks, and, on several napkins, she'd scribbled options.

Duo names fell into categories: the pun (Wight Nights), the verb (Blitz, Jammin'), the tropical (Sea Breeze, Bay Breeze, Salt and Lime), the suggestive (Rapture, Leather and Lace), the jazzy (Satin Dolls, A-Train), and the dual (Double Duty, Double Pleasure, Two's Company).

Band names could be slightly more risqué (Deep Urge, One Night Stand). Bands usually consisted of two couples, in some form or other. In Abu Dhabi, their friends Angie and Todd had joined forces with Steph and Izzie to form Bittersweet. Near the end of their six-month contract, Todd found Izzie and Angie "rehearsing" in the pool cabana. Todd promptly divorced Angie (he said "I divorce you" three times, as was the Emirati custom) and took a gig in Muscat as a solo pianist. Steph went back to England and got her real estate license. Angie and Izzie remained in Abu Dhabi as a duo (Lock and Key).

There were other risks, regardless of band size, Karla knew. "The seven deadlies," Flynn called them, which would be an interesting name for a seven-piece. Lust was obvious, as were gluttony and sloth. The hotel food, the constant booze—you turned soft and round, you didn't fit into your leather pants anymore but kept wearing them. You slept in and found it harder and harder to make it to the gym or the pool, where you'd see people you didn't want to see (the General Manager doing his treadmill laps, the drunk pilot who'd requested "Love in an Elevator" the night before). It was so easy to become pale, unless you made a real effort each day to roll out of bed, slip on the swimwear, drag yourself to a pool lounger, and tan for an hour or two.

Karla had lost weight. The nightly brain-circling song stress contributed, as did boredom with the Continental Cafe menu. She was hungry only after work, and only for veggie buns.

Avarice, pride—you began to buy things, nice things. You had cash to burn—no rent, no food bills, few drinks to pay for yourself. You went to the gold market in Dubai or, Karla had heard, Electronic City in Japan. You wore shiny watches, designer clothes. You treated yourself to a new microphone, an upgraded guitar. In Thailand you could fill entire suitcases with Christmas presents and send them back home via cargo.

In Dubai, Karla purchased expensive rhinestone stud earrings in twelve different shades, colors to match every outfit. She loved them, her pretty rainbow assortment, hard as candy. She thought carefully about which shade to wear each night. She mixed it up sometimes, pale pink with her yellow satin blouse.

That left envy and wrath, which would have to come later.

✧

THE WORLD CUP began, and Karla received a play-off chart to study.

"You'll enjoy it more if you understand the teams," Jack said. He wanted to stay up for the England versus Romania match. It was going to be aired in the hotel staff canteen at 3:00 A.M.

After work, Karla ducked into bed quickly. She needed sleep. She didn't want to wonder if this was where he was really going.

Jack picked up his acoustic, to kill time. He played "Stuck in the Middle with You" and "Carolina in My Mind," and Karla, groggy from the NyQuil she didn't need to be taking anymore, couldn't help but think of the ship's Kiddie Room, when her voice was still new and clear.

She almost woke herself to join in. Almost. But maybe this was what he preferred right now, singing without her.

She felt a tight resentment spread at the thought of this.

At 5:00 A.M. he returned: England lost, 2 to 1. Last few seconds of the bloody game. Karla absorbed this information from somewhere in the depths and slowly turned away from him.

KARLA WALKED back from the library and blocked out the rush hour sounds with her taped lessons. Beth's voice said,

"1998 is *yi jiu jiu ba nian*." It helped to walk and listen, with people who spoke this language streaming past. Karla hated numbers. She still couldn't count to ten. Beth had been kind but firm: Karla needed to practice.

As Beth's voice droned on, Karla saw a woman lean down and blow snot from her left nostril into a square hole in the pavement. *Was the hole there for that purpose?* The woman wiped her fingers on the sidewalk, straightened up, and walked on.

Karla rewound the tape. *Concentrate.* It was terrible to feel dumb.

She was not dumb. Just distracted. Nerves, the snot woman, getting in the way.

KARLA WAS READY for her next lesson. Jack gathered his squash things and prepared to leave them alone.

"I think she is very clever," said Beth, for Jack.

"She seems to think so, too," said Jack, smiling just in time.

With Jack safely out of the room, Beth confided. There was a boy, just a friend. She wanted to take him for a walk. She wasn't being metaphorical. She wanted to ask him herself, but her girlfriends said she shouldn't. "It isn't the typical Chinese way," Beth explained, "for the girl to ask."

Karla gave her carpe diem spiel. (Beth asked her to write this down, both *carpe diem* and *spiel.*) She told Beth to follow her heart. Life was short.

"I think this is good advice," said Beth.

These are bad clichés, Karla knew. *And I am the worst hypocrite ever.*

✧

IF KARLA WAS going to apply to the Portland School of Art, she needed to finish her application essay. She was supposed to explain why art school appealed to her, why photography appealed to her, but she had no idea why. She wanted to photograph Willow and Jack and Willow's shoes from Marcello, but she didn't know how to make these things seem fluid and important in a snapshot frame.

Instead she spent the day with Margaret, constructing *qi paos* from scratch—red, silky material and spiral buttons and steep slits and matching handbags and lots of body parts measured by a tailor's tape. They had coffee in the Empire Hotel lobby when they were done, and then wandered in the thick heat to the secret apartment Margaret shared with her Japanese boyfriend.

"Don't tell the colleagues!" she warned, as she opened the door with her key. "They think I'm a rich girl. And don't tell *him* about the *qi pao*. His money."

But the boyfriend was asleep in the bedroom with the door shut. Karla and Margaret sat on a black leather couch drinking orange juice from squat glasses as quietly as possible. There were six remote controls on the coffee table. There was a wine rack in the kitchen. The floors were lined with pastel tiles, and sweet AC rushed in from angled ceiling vents.

Margaret sat rigidly, as though waiting in a dentist's office.

"I've been here with him one year already," she whispered. She seemed worried about this.

Karla wanted to ask many things, but it was impossible. They finished their juice, boyfriend-conscious. Karla made excuses and got in a taxi.

At the hotel she e-mailed her parents, trimmed her toe-nails, and plucked five stray eyebrow hairs. Then it was time for dinner and work.

✧

IN AUGUST, President Clinton visited, and the traffic on Zhong Lu was blocked, the sidewalk bulging with crowds behind stanchions. Karla and Jack joined in and took many blurry pictures of the limo as it passed. Karla saw a fluff of Chelsea's hair and someone's hand, waving. Jack saw *him*. Or so he said. Although Jack had never admitted it, Karla knew he admired Clinton's confident jaw, his twinkle. He could probably tell a good joke. He was the guy in the pub everyone wanted to be near.

They sat in the Long Bar for two hours, across from the Portman Hotel. The Palace concierge had given them a tip-off; they were the only ones there.

"But how do we know he'll come out?" Karla needed to work on her application.

"Maybe he won't," said Jack. But it seemed promising—the limo was parked outside.

When the president finally emerged, Karla nearly missed him—she'd been mopping up spilled beer on the floor with a frustratingly thin napkin—but Jack gave a yelp, and she caught him just in time: one solid flash of the famous profile before he ducked into the limo.

Karla was excited by it all, despite herself. She mentioned it on the mike that night, apropos of nothing, before Jack could.

After work, on the couch, they watched shots of Shang-hai on BBC World.

"I'm glad we did that today," she said.

"Stick with me."

"I don't usually do that."

"What, see the president? I wouldn't think so."

"I mean, wait for famous people to appear. It's a little..."
Tacky, she thought.

"Common?" He kept his eyes on the TV.

"Impolite," she said. "But you make me do things."

"I don't make you do anything," he said.

"No— I mean, you make me do things I don't usually do.
It's a good thing." When Jack's parents had come to visit in
Dubai, he'd insisted Karla wear the Emirati national dress to
the airport with him. It had worried her, but she knew there
was no talking him out of it. It was like going to Jamaica in a
dreadlock wig, she thought. Would they offend someone?
Would they be asked to remove their robes?

But nothing happened. They were ignored by everyone,
except Jack's parents, who cackled and gave them kisses and
then asked to be taken to the closest pub.

"God bless America," said Jack. "God bless Bill." He was
diverting her; he didn't like this kind of flattery. But she knew
he was grateful.

WILLOW WAS PUT on probation for a week, for "inappropriate
behavior." She'd told Sam to "go fuck the mother." Karla felt
somewhat responsible.

For the next six nights, Willow came just as Jack and
Karla finished their last set. (Jim the doorman let her sneak
through the lobby.) She wasn't allowed inside the bar, so she
lingered just beyond the entrance, by the elevator. In her real

clothes—pastel blouses, cotton skirts, her famous Marcello shoes—she looked much older. The waitresses gave her cigarettes and Willow looked sweetly rebellious, laughing through the glass, making faces at Margaret, plucking flowers from the nearest arrangement and pinning them to her close-cropped hair. Sam remained steely-eyed.

✧

KARLA BOUGHT another pair of shoes. "*Qī*," she said, and it worked—out came size seven.

THEY WENT to a new place called Rhino with an Irish bartender and a few bored expats watching a prerecorded World Cup game. The walls were yellow and red, and the tables were small geometrical shapes that were impossible to balance plates on. Karla's fries landed on the floor and had to be replaced. They had sweet drinks that didn't taste particularly strong. Jack finished hers.

Jack said, "What's wrong?"

Karla said, "I'm not sure. The Sunday blues. A little homesick, maybe."

Jack laughed at this, which seemed odd. He said, "I think I'm going mad."

So Karla laughed, but he kept saying it. "I'm going mad." And then, "I think I'm having a panic attack."

Karla stopped laughing.

"I can't think straight," Jack said. "It's not funny." His pupils were large. "What would you do?" he asked. "Where would you take me if something went wrong? Would you know what to do?"

"I'd take you to the hospital if it got too bad," Karla said. "But it won't, you'll be okay." She asked for the check. She held on to his hand.

"But you wouldn't know where to go. You don't speak Chinese."

"Neither do you," she reminded him, then remembered the shoes. "But I ordered shoes," she said. *Ordered* was the wrong word. "In Chinese."

"I don't speak Chinese, either. Where would you take me?" Then his head was on the table. "Let's go. We have to go," he said.

In the taxi, Jack's eyes were closed and he said nothing. Karla told him the only two jokes she could remember: A guy walks into a bar and says, "Ouch." And, a Buddhist walks up to a hot dog vendor and says, "Make me one with everything."

"I might be dying," Jack said. His lips looked dry.

She told him he wasn't dying. "It'll be gone in the morning," she said. She thought of what they'd consumed: soup, fries, sandwich, vodka, Coke. Nothing had tasted poisonous. And then Karla began to feel it too, hyperaware and hypersensitive. *Hyper, hyper, hyper,* she thought. It felt nice. She forgot to be bothered by what he'd said: *You wouldn't know what to do.*

It took a very long time for the elevator to reach their room, and then Jack tumbled onto the bed without undressing and was out within minutes.

Karla laughed as she brushed her teeth. She remembered to fill two tall glasses with water. She drank both, refilled them, and brought them to his side.

"You must drink these now," she said. She was fairly certain she'd said it out loud. She said it again, just to be sure.

He roused himself and sipped a little. "I never want to

feel like this again," he said, exactly four times. He slept, and then she did, too.

At 5:00 A.M., she woke up and sat upright with an odd, gummy taste in her mouth. She watched the TV clock spin and spin until she made it stop.

When Jack woke up, he was fine but groggy. Neither of them had a drop to drink that night.

In future retellings, someone had slipped ecstasy into their drinks. In China, of all places! The bartender was Irish, Jack would say. The tables were ridiculously small, Karla would remember. *It felt amazing,* she would think. *And he didn't trust me at all.*

✧

JACK AND KARLA fought onstage about the foot-pedal reverb switch, which Karla kept forgetting to turn off between songs, which made Jack's voice echo. It was on her side of the stage; it was her responsibility. Jack had suddenly decided, with little Sky Bar time remaining, to speak on the mike.

"Get it together," he hissed.

"Fuck off," she hissed back.

The guests didn't suspect a thing. Or so Jack and Karla told themselves.

After work, there was yet another late World Cup game. Jack came in at 4:06 A.M., and by 7:00 A.M., Karla still couldn't sleep. She drank a Tsingtao in the bathroom to stop her brain from spinning and listened to Paul Simon on headphones, the one about life getting better and a train sounding hopefully, persistently in the distance.

Maybe it was true—maybe they would be better somewhere else. A new adventure, a brand-new venue. And if she got into the Portland School of Art, she'd have something else to do. She'd photograph artful scenes in artful light. She'd begin to have her own career. Something like JOE, but better.

✧

THEY WENT to the beer garden at O'Farley's, which was crowded and muggy. Karla had four halves of Guinness and an Irish coffee and no food. The trio began to play, and Jack spoke to them during their break. Karla spoke, too, and conversation came easily. (The fiddler had returned to Shannon, but the accordion player remembered her from Heaven, from Finnish Night.) But then Karla stood and tripped, and Jack placed a bottle of Evian in her hand and told her to drink it.

"Take me home," she said. "Country roads."

"Easy," said Jack.

Karla heard her sandals scraping along the sidewalk, and then they were home and Jack took off the very same sandals and pushed her into bed.

"We'll talk later," Karla said, shooing him away, and slept for hours, good Guinness pumping through her blood. She woke once and thought, *I don't give a shit about anything right now,* and in the morning, for nearly a minute, she was able to sustain the feeling. *How lovely! Nothing to worry about!* And she understood for the first time why Jack drank so much. She just hadn't been drinking *enough.*

THE WINDOW cleaners woke her, beyond the thick curtains, perched outside the eighteenth floor. They made strange tapping and rubbing sounds, and before waking Karla had thought for sure that someone—Jack or a bellboy—was in-

side the room, scratching at the beige walls, making fingerprints. She had to wake herself and find out for sure.

But no one was there. And so she slept again, and dreamed
she was opening the door. Mail—lots of it! Stamps from Maine
and postcards and magazines scattered at her feet.

The cleaners' platform lurched loudly.

And then her canine tooth snapped off and she rushed to
the sink, bleeding. Her tongue was stained red, and she rinsed
and rinsed in the sink, closing the stopper so she wouldn't
lose any tooth pieces. She grinned in order to see the damage:
terrible, jagged smile. How would she work? It was *real*, it happened! A gaping, bloody hole where her tooth had been.

She woke, and there was sweet, solid enamel there instead. It was 1:33 P.M.

She made herself sit upright—the dream was too un-
pleasant. In the shower she dropped the soap three times. She
spooned Nescafé into her cup but forgot the water and tried
to sip the coffee grains.

She had become a very bad sitcom character.

✧

THEY WERE on the second verse of "Englishman in New York"
when the Lady in Green appeared again. At first Karla thought
she was laughing and that the glass had fallen from the bar by
accident. But then she smashed another against the marble
tiles by the bar, and then another, random drinks from random
people around her. She was wailing, not laughing. She was
slapping at the air and clinging to the back of a man's shirt.

Willow, no longer on probation, stood with her hand
over her mouth. Jack kept singing. (*"A gentleman will walk*

but never run…") And then the big bouncer from the lobby arrived and steered the Lady in Green away.

But Karla could still see her through the glass door, crawling on the carpet by the elevator, squirming and screaming until the bouncer lifted her up by the waist and hugged her from behind. Her dress was hiked up, and her lacy underwear looked white from where Karla stood, not green.

"Wacko," said Jack, as the Sting song faded, as the Lady in Green disappeared behind elevator doors.

SAM RAISED his glass of Heineken. "You are my best friend," he said. He was still in his uniform. The last guest had left two hours ago, and the doors were locked. "My very best friend."

He didn't mean Jack. He meant his beer.

Jack chuckled, and Karla knew he would quote this forever. Karla drank chardonnay, slowly. She'd had enough, but she wanted to finish what was in her glass. It seemed right.

Earlier that night, Sam said, he'd told a Canadian guest that the tequila was out of stock. The guest had scowled.

"Sorry, sir," Sam had said. He'd unfolded the sharp end of his pocket corkscrew and presented it to the man. "Here is the knife. You want to kill me?"

And the guy had laughed and ordered a Tsingtao instead.

"You're on a roll tonight," Jack said.

"I think so," said Sam.

"A Canadian?" said Karla. "Maybe it was Sid the Comedian."

Jack looked at Karla and then looked at his beer. "Sid the schmuck?"

"He jumped ship," said Karla. *He knew when to leave, at least.*

Sam noticed a stray shard on the carpet and bent to retrieve it.

"She didn't seem all there," said Karla. "Something very bad must have happened."

"Who are you talking about?" said Jack.

"The Green Lady. The Lady in Green."

"We're not talking about her anymore."

"We should be," said Karla.

"She is not a welcome guest here," Sam said. And then, "We should drink more. My friend has left me now." His glass was empty. Jack laughed and Karla, filled with wine, excused herself.

IN THE MORNING, Karla thought about things she preferred not to think about.

1. Jack was wearing a yellow shirt with small white buttons, and three buttons popped off. She was standing by a Dumpster in Dubai, stacked cardboard in piles in the sand, and she was screaming. She couldn't actually feel her fingers, but she knew she was clawing at his shirt, ripping, and the three buttons flew and landed somewhere near the Dumpster. (In the morning the cardboard would be gathered by someone and tied together with string for money. Maybe a button would be found.) Hot night air and sand grinding between the pavement and her heels. People in nearby apartments could hear them, she was aware of this, but it didn't make her stop. Jack

held her wrists together. And then he dropped her wrists, disgusted. He turned his back and walked up the street, back to the bar she'd stormed from, and she was left there to yell at him as he walked away from her.

The next day she sewed three buttons back on, using spares from her travel sewing kit. (The shirt had been balled and thrown on the floor at 6:00 A.M., when Jack returned.) The buttons didn't match very well and he would never wear the shirt again, but she had fixed it, at least. He would even thank her, without malice, months later, when it was safe to do so, over a drink in a neutral bar where they'd never had a fight before.

Earlier, she thought she'd seen his hand linger on the thigh of a Welsh girl with enormous lips. They were there with a big group—twelve or so, all spread out over barstools and a few small tables, and Karla was mingling, high—she looked over at him and his hand was there, on the stranger's thigh. She was sure of it.

2. In Dubai, Jack started taking spinning classes, and the instructor came to their bar alone and she was British, with perfectly toned arms, and she teased Jack as though she'd known him for years. Karla excused herself and spent twenty-five minutes in the bathroom. When she returned, Jack was already back onstage. Their break had been too long and the Bar Manager had complained and where the fuck did she disappear to, anyway? The spinning instructor was gone and Karla felt much better.

3. In Muscat she had read, though she knew it was terrible, Jack's diary. Just one line of one random entry, but it was

the worst possible one: "I woke up wanting to, badly, but not with her." It was dated five months earlier.

4. She did tequila shots and yelled, "Just fucking love me, just love me, fucker, motherfucker, fucking *love* me!" and he tucked her in and never mentioned it again.

5. She discovered, from Glo, that Jack had taken Flynn to a hostess bar instead of a World Cup game. They hadn't done anything, Glo said, breezily. They'd just talked to girls. Just to see what it was like in there.

"New York Bar or something."

"Gotham Bar," Karla said.

"Jack took him. He'd never been there before. I just thought you should know. Who cares, right?" Glo's breeziness was fading a little.

"Actually," she said to Glo, "Flynn took *him* there." This was an outright lie. "That's what Jack said. But who cares, right? They're just being boys."

She felt better for exactly three minutes, at which point regret began to seep in. She bought Glo a margarita and watched as she downed it in seconds.

6. She felt the bed shaking and was instantly awake. It was morning, just before the TV alarm was scheduled to go off.

What was she supposed to do? Sit bolt upright and say, *What am I, chopped liver?*

She stayed very still, her heart very loud, until it was over. She could smell it, beneath the sheets. And minutes later, when he was in the shower, where he was probably doing it again, she patted the bed down with her palm and felt the damp patch.

In a way, she was relieved. *Evidence.* She wasn't completely insane.

7. She once called him a jerk, and he wouldn't speak to her until dinner.

"Don't ever. Ever. Call me that. Again."

"What?"

"Don't be fucking cute."

"What's your problem? I called you a jerk. It means nothing."

"You know what it means."

"It means nothing. I'm American. *American.* I know my fucking language. It means nothing!" But she couldn't manage to convince him.

They still had certain lapses in language like that. She'd said *frigging* once, and he'd looked at her in shock.

"That's ladylike."

"*Fuck* is worse."

"It isn't. *Frig* is...nasty. You *never* say that."

"It's not. *Fuck* is worse."

And so on.

She started calling him a jerk again, once the wet patches appeared. She understood what it meant to him now.

8. He sometimes said, when she was in a bad mood, "What's wrong with your face?" He meant, "Get happy. Get rid of your sneer, your ugliness."

"Nothing's wrong with it," she snapped. But she worried. Did her face look unhappy? Was this permanent?

In high school, Karla's prom date, Randall Page, had called her effervescent. She shimmered, he said. It wasn't just the pot speaking. She was smiley and golden, with her long hair in honey-colored curls. She would spread goodness and joy, wherever she went.

But it was gone. The goodness had been replaced, and people could actually see it. Something was wrong with her face.

✧

AT DINNER, Karla brought her up again, the Lady in Green. She needed to know.

"Did you find it scary?" she asked Jack. "Her reaction?" She picked at her shrimp cocktail and didn't look at him.

"Yeah," said Jack, watching Karla. "Very much so."

"It's an awful feeling, to be that mad at someone."

"She was pissed, Karla. She had to be. She wasn't right."

She looked up. "Or," she said, "she just wanted someone to see her."

✧

BECAUSE THE aerobics class was canceled, Karla and Margaret jogged next to each other on treadmills for fifteen minutes and then went to the Orient Shopping Center. In the café, Margaret ordered blueberry iced tea, and Karla asked for apple juice.

"I feel sad," Margaret said, "but not for me."

Karla prodded gently.

Willow was causing trouble again, said Margaret, after one week back.

"Trouble for Sam?" Karla asked.

"Trouble for Sam, for me. I been there four years already. I'm ten years older than her—than Willow. Willow is a silly girl."

Karla nodded, feeling disloyal. Margaret was good at her job, good at listening to boring drunks. She was friendly and welcoming without being too flirtatious. She knew how to make strangers happy.

Karla was about to say this to Margaret, or a version of it, when Margaret blurted, "Willow is pregnant." Margaret looked at her blue drink as she spoke. "I know this. Two months already."

"Mr. Marcello?" Karla asked. *That bastard.*

Margaret shrugged.

IT WAS RAINING when they left the café, big, fat drops, and so Karla hailed a taxi. By the time the door was shut, the sky had opened and everyone outside was soaked. It was a sudden, lovely gift, coolness after days of gray heat. The drops were loud, metallic, and Karla was safe inside.

Willow, at work, said, "Outside is big rain."

Don't have the baby, Karla thought. She looked carefully at the waist of Willow's *qi pao,* which was still perfectly flat.

Later, during the break, she found Willow in the ladies' room, peeing with the door wide open, girlish pink underwear around her ankles. "Ka-la!" she said.

Karla wondered if this would be her lasting image of Willow: squatting, oblivious, flashing a smile so gorgeous you had to smile back. You wanted to be the object of that smile. You'd do almost anything for it.

✧

KARLA TRIED AGAIN to be sober for the night. It gave her something to focus on, a way to block out distractions onstage. Jack was one such distraction. They were fighting again. Yelling and slamming doors. Jack had skipped dinner, and Karla had been too upset to read.

But it was good for singing—mild, focused anger. It made Karla less afraid. She wanted to belt, and belting was easier with a solid, steely base at her center.

By the third set she'd calmed down. She'd given in and had a glass of wine. She allowed her mind to drift as she sang.

The song ended, and Jack started another. The Eagles disc was in, and she knew he'd let it play to the end: "Tequila Sunrise" followed by "Life in the Fast Lane" followed by "Lyin' Eyes."

Karla had a calendar in her mind, and she checked off the days. She saw the flag of September 24, their Shanghai Palace departure date.

They would travel for ten days after their last day of work, before flying home. This would be their vacation, or working vacation—Jack had arranged several JOE appointments in each stop: Beijing, Shenzhen, Hong Kong. They'd decided this would be more exciting than Dubai.

Once home, they'd wait for word from Liza. She'd promised nothing but had hinted at Japan or "maybe, *maybe*," the Caribbean.

It was easier that way, easier than figuring out what they really wanted to do.

"Lyin' Eyes" came on, and Karla tried to calculate: They'd sung that song…many, many times.

When it was over, Karla clicked off the reverb switch and unscrewed her microphone from its stand. She put in the most benign CD she could find, Sade, and pressed Play.

Jack watched her closely.

He's going to apologize. He's going to propose. He's going to ask for a divorce.

"Heaven?" he said. "I fancy quesadillas."

"Sure," she said, coolly.

And they were friends again, just like that.

✧

THEY MET JASMINE—Jason and Minnie—the next Sky Bar duo, who arrived on Jack and Karla's last night of work. The Northern Lights photo had already been replaced. Jasmine flyers were artfully fanned on the reception desk and planted in each hotel room. Minnie wore a tight blue dress in the picture, and before she'd arrived Willow had announced, "Her arms very fat." Karla didn't disagree.

"They have a good duo name," she'd said.

Jack and Karla's last night in the Sky Bar was much like the 191 nights before. Jason and Minnie kept their distance and clapped politely from the back of the room. They were speaking to Sam and laughing. Willow and Margaret had already introduced themselves. Minnie was wearing an orchid in her hair that Willow had plucked from a bouquet.

No one else could come to see Karla and Jack on their last night; they were all working. But they'd seen Gin Fizz and Steve and Tammy at Heaven one last time. Flynn, getting over the flu, was sedate. Glo took their address down carefully with a purple pen. The Long Island iced teas were on the house, and Tammy prepared extra-spicy quesadillas. The Finn strolled by and, seeing Flynn, refused to come inside.

Beth, on summer vacation in Sichuan, sent a letter to Karla as promised. Her prose was grammatically perfect. She wanted to study abroad, maybe in Boston. Could they keep in touch?

After their last aerobics class, Margaret gave Karla a small notebook, leather bound, with the Chinese character for happiness stamped on each page.

And now, after their last song in Shanghai, "Don't It Make My Brown Eyes Blue," Sam presented Jack and Karla with a bottle of Dom Pérignon.

"We must drink it right now," said Sam. And they did, plus many more bottles of the cheaper stuff.

Willow kissed them both (she'd had a full glass of Dom herself), and then called the next morning when Jack was in the shower.

"I miss you!" she said.

Karla hadn't yet mentioned it, and she wanted to. "Willow," she said. "I know what happened. You're going to be fine."

"Everything's okay," she said. She giggled.

"I mean, your baby."

"I know, Ka-la. Baby." And that was all. Her voice was certain, decisive. *"Leave me alone,"* she meant.

FOR WEEKS Karla had envisioned their last, poignant meander through the marble lobby.

There was no meander. It was more like a fast clip. They were late; the airport bus was waiting. And Jack wanted to avoid the two-hundred-dollar bar bill they had yet to settle.

There was no one there to see them off, not even Jason or Minnie, who were already sightseeing. No time for final photographs.

Jack and Karla had stayed up until five packing the equipment, labeling things, shellacking tape onto cracks and holes

188 ◆ LARA TUPPER

of amp covers and speakers. The gear would make its own way back to York, leaving China before them, arriving in the UK after. They left it there for the bellboys and were unhindered.

But not really. In the airport they checked a ridiculous amount of personal luggage and had six carry-ons between them. They wandered around the terminal, slow from the heat, unable to find their gate, as though they had never done this before. The back of Jack's shirt was dark with sweat, and his brow was dented with annoyance.

"We don't have to sing tonight," Karla reminded him. "Or the next night, or the next."

He attempted a smile. "I'm trying to think of a pun, something about Northern Lights no longer appearing."

"A meteorological hiatus," Karla offered. "Due to atmospheric differences."

"More like 'A break from the limelight.'"

"A well-deserved break," Karla said. Her backpack straps were digging in.

TWELVE

Willie Nelson

IN BEIJING THEY stayed at the Fiesta Resort, several miles from the city center. The F and B Manager, whom Jack had befriended in the Sky Bar, had wanted to hear "Twist and Shout." In return, Jack and Karla received an extremely discounted rate and drink vouchers for the pool bar.

They checked in and used the vouchers on tepid cans of Heineken, watching as Dutch children threw themselves from a sturdy blue diving board. The silence between Jack and Karla was long and comfortable. Karla's muscles ached from lugging.

After a lengthy shower, Karla put on a mint-colored Fiesta robe and quietly slapped her bare feet against the waxed, wooden floorboards. She combed her wet hair and tucked herself under the crisp duvet for a nap. *Four Weddings and a Funeral* was on TV, the volume low. The twin beds were divided by a small, neat bureau.

Jack prepared JOE portfolios, sliding copies of pictures and résumés into heavy plastic sheaths.

I haven't felt this calm in months, Karla thought. She slept as though a large brick had been slammed into her head, painlessly. *The relief of separate beds.*

THAT NIGHT, the Food and Beverage Manager arranged for them to have a free meal in Henry J. Beans, housed in the hotel, and there they received VIP treatment. (A small sign had been placed at their table: RESERVED FOR THE VIP.) Jack handed out cards to the Bar Manager, the pianist, the Head Waiter, and the busboy. The Eagles came on when the pianist took his break, "Life in the Fast Lane."

"It's nice to hear the songs without having to sing the words," Karla said. Jack sang along anyway.

In the Beijing Hard Rock Cafe, they had overpriced manhattans. There was no band that night, so they drank quickly. Jack passed out more cards.

In the Hard Rock Arcade next door, two boys played a game involving robots and rocks; the robots hurled giant rocks at one another until one robot was unable to get back up. Karla started giggling and couldn't stop—the quick manhattan, the Long Island iced tea at dinner. And the game was so stupid and the boys didn't know they had an audience and it just seemed so pointless. *Rocks! Robots!* Karla was crying with laughter, her stomach clenched in a happy knot.

Jack laughed, too, but he didn't mean it. He propped himself on her shoulder, as though he needed support. He pretended to be a robot, shielding himself from rocks. It was what they should be doing, laughing together, relieved of normal duties, falling back into something that would stick.

THE NEXT DAY they were early for their 9:00 A.M. bus, sleepy but willing. They'd booked the tour weeks ago through the

Palace concierge: The Great Wall! This was something their parents could tell people, something tangible to report.

At 9:15 Karla had a terrible, sinking feeling. She looked at their tickets and realized.

She'd fucked up. They were one day late.

Jack reverted to Ents. Team mode as Karla played the panicky tourist. He called the Palace concierge, and an hour later they were on a private tour in a private car with a Chinese guide (Sue) and a nameless driver, heading to Badaling.

Karla tried not to be cranky anymore. He'd fixed it.

The drive was long and so they dozed, squashed in the back of the small sedan. Sue woke them in time to see the first views of the wall, twisting, winding, authentically medieval. Or was it? They were ready; they had their questions prepared.

Jack went first. "Why was it built?"

Karla added more words. Why all the bother and why is it such a snakelike thing, doubling back and forth and taking unseemly ninety-degree turns and how old is it, exactly, and what about the deaths? We want to know about the deaths.

Because, said Sue, there were complicated borders and pesky, warring Mongolians. There were guards at checkpoint towers, shooting arrows. There were dead builders buried along the way, and their bones were found much later among crumbling sections of wall.

This was good, very good. Jack hugged Karla a little and sang the Paul Simon song as the driver parked and locked the car.

Sue took their picture, with the eight turrets in the background. Most visitors climbed four, she said, but the best view was from the eighth. They could take the path to the right, the one crowded with walkers, or they could turn left, where the path was steep and deserted.

Right, Jack and Karla agreed. They wanted people.

Sue waved and waited at the bottom to smoke cigarettes with the driver. They had two hours.

There were vendors at every turn, selling postcards and T-shirts, red with black print, I CLIMBED THE GREAT WALL, and certificates with the same statement, and magnets and coonskin caps. There were camels parked at certain points for photo ops, chewing from side to side. Jack chewed from side to side.

At the archery stand, Jack bought ten arrows for ten yuan. He shot two before Karla looked over the wall to the targets below, camouflaged among the bushes—rabbits, real ones, surrounded by stray yellow arrows, their paws tied to poles. If you hit a bunny, you could take it home, the vendor mimed, seeing Karla's expression. "Dinner," he said, smiling.

Karla yanked Jack away, and he swore he hadn't seen them, the bunnies. They saw occasional plastic bags after that, carried by fathers, with dead rabbits inside.

"I should have lived back then," Jack said, to change the subject.

She tried to imagine Jack aiming at Mongolians but couldn't.

"Life was dangerous. Men lived," he said. She knew what he meant. He liked the idea of swords and codpieces, of simpler violence.

They passed through the first of the towers, a cool and shaded wind trap. The tourists were Chinese and Japanese and German and Australian. A girl in platform shoes struggled up the steep part, and little kids needed boosts up the steps. But everyone made it somehow. They smiled and pushed on and posed for picture after picture, waiting patiently for good shots between crowds of heads.

The view, as Sue had said, was better as Jack and Karla continued to climb. In parts there were no steps, just steep, slippery grades, shiny from millions of passing feet. In the distance they saw disconnected portions of wall—ruined and sprouting trees. Portions cut off from them.

"What a paranoid bunch of emperors," said Karla. "To build this thing."

Jack said he was glad they had. He wished his mam could see.

They decided it was one of the seven wonders. They guessed at what the others might be. Jack said the wall was the only man-made thing visible from space because it was built on small mountain peaks, and the peaks alone would probably be visible from space.

"It's a misleading fact then," Karla said.

They'd been dawdling—too much time shooting rabbits—and now they only had time to make it to Tower 7. What was she going to *tell* people? Jack asked, all the way down.

But it really did bother her. She couldn't shake it. *We didn't have time,* she'd have to explain. *There were eight towers, but we only made it to seven. It wasn't our fault—we had to get back. We had to meet Sue.*

The drive back to the hotel was a sleepy blur of mountainside and sky.

NEXT: Shenzhen, and more JOE meetings. And then Hong Kong.

Karla shopped during Jack's appointments. In HMV

Music she scanned the CDs greedily and bought something by Third Eye Blind, a band she'd never heard of. The streets were clean and the sidewalks were wide. Versace and Armani labels everywhere, no rickshaws or laundry lines, not as far as Karla could see. She sat on a marble bench near a fountain and began to fill out postcards.

"Clear water, green hills in the distance. Like Hawaii," Karla wrote to her parents. She'd never been to Hawaii, and her parents knew this, but they would know what she meant.

Jasmine were flying to Hawaii in fourteen months to get married. Eight months in Shanghai, followed by six months in Tokyo—they'd already signed their next contract. And from Tokyo, straight to Honolulu. They'd announced this in the Sky Bar. Minnie already had the ring.

"Hawaii—wow," Karla had said. "It's in good proximity." *Proximity?* She could have said, "It's close by—that'll be an easy flight," or "Good for you! That will be beautiful."

Later she'd said to Jack, "They certainly like to plan ahead." And then, "Her ring is really small."

THAT NIGHT they went to Victoria Peak, a "must-see." The line for the tram was long, but eventually they boarded and zipped up at a sharp angle, pressed close together on a smooth wooden bench.

The view from the top was worth it, Jack admitted. He squeezed Karla's waist. The towers glittered and changed color: red to yellow to green to blue, not in a flashy neon way but dimming fluidly from one shade to the next. The air was warm, the tourists buzzed in and out of restaurants and stores, and the dancing fountain did just that. Karla and Jack ate soup and sandwiches in an outdoor café, and there, unbelievably, saw Sonny the Blues Man and Wanda, his Lady Friend.

They paid quickly and took the tram straight down. The descent shoved them hard against the wooden bench.

"We're awful," said Karla.

"We're not," said Jack. "We're on vacation."

And then they were walking across another vast lobby for Jack's last meeting of the day.

Three champagne tables in the back paid for the entire bar, the Irish F and B explained, after buying them drinks.

Karla pretended not to hear. It was her job to be quiet, to smile, like being on stage.

Did Jack have a band of champagne caliber?

Jack did, absolutely. He would send a portfolio first thing next week.

Irish shook Jack's hand and nodded to Karla and left them to nurse the remaining bottle of Merlot.

"Champagne caliber!" Karla hissed, sipping. "He didn't really say that."

"We have to stay and finish this," Jack said. Merlot wasn't his favorite. "And I have fuck-all to send him."

"Was I a good, quiet little girlfriend?" Karla was feeling the wine.

"You were," he said. "Thank you."

They refilled their glasses and listened to the band—European, cabaret-ish, with a charismatic Italian singer and a horn section. A seven-piece! But they already had a name: Eureka. Thirteen people listened attentively (Karla counted). The band played as though hundreds were there.

The wine was gone. They hurried to catch the last subway back to Kowloon, and it all seemed like a fabulous adventure to Karla, running along Hong Kong streets, Jack leading the way, clutching her hand. "Careful," he kept saying.

Of what? The traffic? The darkness? Each other? She didn't care just then, but she would in the morning: They didn't have long. They'd be home soon. They were running out of time.

KARLA CHECKED her e-mail while Jack copied résumés in the Business Center. Her mother had written to say she'd received a letter from the Portland School of Art. Should she open it?

If Karla got in, she'd have to go back to Maine for the orientation. She'd have to meet her professors and buy her supplies.

She'd have something that was hers and not his.

Not yet, Karla replied. *Please,* she added.

MORE APPOINTMENTS, even though it was their very last day.

After the first (InterContinental), they wandered along Nathan Road, searching for a cheap place to eat. Instead, they found a small clothing store with a precise, pale blue dress in the window. The material was shiny and vaguely Asian— faint bamboo leaves in an unobtrusive pattern. It was knee-length, sleeveless, and came with a perfect matching purse.

Karla bought it quickly, greedily, damn the price. The cashier told them to visit the men's shop next door, and within minutes Jack was measured for a cream suit, which would be delivered to the hotel before their flight the next morning.

They skipped the café search, too excited by their purchases. They went to McDonald's.

At night they skipped the hotel bar and bought cans of Carlsberg from the 7-Eleven, then walked along the hotel promenade. They perched close on a flat bench and watched the quarter moon, a bright tangerine slice between the towers. They stared for a long time and said nothing. Music from a lounge somewhere bounced off the shallow stretch of harbor before them.

Jack spoke. "To think it all started in the Kiddie Room."

How many cans had he drunk? Not many. And he wasn't being a smart-ass. He touched her arm, and she felt a reluctant lurch in her chest.

THE NEXT DAY, they boarded a plane at Hong Kong's gleaming, new Chep Lok Kok Airport. Jack took the window. The airplane wing read, "Do not walk outside this area."

"I will not walk outside that area," said Jack, for Karla, and closed his eyes.

IN HER CARRY-ON, Karla had a dog-eared manila envelope packed with notes from the past eight months scrawled on receipts, napkins, Sky Bar request cards. "Blurbs," she'd written, in pencil, in the upper left-hand corner.

As Jack slept, she began to make small piles on the tray table.

Willow says her freckles are from little birds pecking at her cheeks when she was little. Her mother told her so. (Keep.)

Things I've seen carried on bicycles: puppies, hula hoops, blocks of ice as big as TVs (unwrapped and melting very slowly), five HP laser printers in boxes, stacked and twined together. (Keep. She remembered Jack saying, of the printers, "It could be an advert: 'We deliver. Anyhow, anywhere.'")

A sticker in a taxi said, "Don't forget to carry your thing."
(Keep.)

After twenty minutes of sorting she threw away only one:

> *J: What's the matter?*
> *Me: Can't sleep.*
> *J, linking his leg with mine under the covers: Just*
> *close your eyes and hold on, and I'll take you with me.*

It seemed made-up. It had to be.

WHAT SHE DID remember was the thing he'd said that morning, very early. It was six or seven, and he'd burped and sighed and flung a heavy leg over Karla's knees.

"I love you," he said.

This woke her.

"Who's pumpkin soup?" he added.

"You are?" she guessed.

"No. It's *you*." And he promptly disappeared again.

She asked him about it over room service breakfast, to see if he remembered. She buttered her rye toast and asked, "Why did you call me a big fat pumpkin?"

He looked up quickly from the business section. "Pumpkin soup. I dreamed about it."

Karla had ordered it for several days in a row at the Continental Café, before they'd left. It came in a real little pumpkin, carved out.

"It was good," she said, biting a U into the toast. "You should try it next time we're back at the Shanghai Palace."

"It's a Halloween thing. It's not Halloween yet."

"You don't even know Halloween," said Karla. "Guy Fawk?"

"Guy Fawkes."

"Guy Fawkes. Set a guy on fire. What kind of holiday is that?"

He didn't answer, and she refused to ask him about the other thing he'd said.

KARLA WROTE it all down on the vomit bag. This she wanted to keep.

THIRTEEN

Sonny and Cher

THEY LANDED IN Heathrow and took a long, slow train to York. They unpacked, presented gifts, and passed around Karla's photo albums.

Karla claimed a drawer in the guest room, where Jack's mom wanted her to stay, where Jack stored his JOE files. Jack's own room, across the stairwell, still had posters of Frank Sinatra and Newcastle United tacked to pale yellow walls.

WHEN THE EQUIPMENT arrived, they spent an afternoon scrubbing off the duct tape goo with warm, soapy water, which seemed pointless to Karla; they'd only have to do it again when they arrived at the next place.

Jack said, "That's like never washing dishes because they just get dirty again."

It wasn't, actually, but Karla didn't want to argue. And so they stacked the clean guitar cases and speakers and amps in his parents' garage and waited for Liza to call.

On Sunday afternoons, Jack's mother cooked dinner for

eight. Jack's brothers came with their wives, and each time they had roast beef, Yorkshire puddings, butternut squash, Brussels sprouts, mashed potatoes, cauliflower with cheese, and Cadbury ice-cream bars. The wives and Karla washed dishes, and everyone else claimed their designated spots in the living room to watch soccer or reruns of *Absolutely Fabulous* or to read sections from the *Times*.

When Jack's cell phone rang on the third Sunday afternoon, Karla had already fallen asleep in a floral armchair, the arts section spread on her lap. She thought, in her bloated, blurry state, that it must be Liza calling from Japan or Australia or wherever she was negotiating work for them next. In fact, Karla knew, Liza lived in nearby Scunthorpe and did all her negotiating via fax.

It wasn't Liza. It was Willow! Jack said her name out loud and smiled at once.

Karla forced her head up. *Willow, in her black* qi pao, *sitting on the peanut room bucket.*

Jack's mother mouthed, "Who is it?"

"Don't," Jack said, into the phone. And then, "I think maybe you should call back another time," in a way that wasn't a suggestion.

She'd begged for his cell number before leaving, Jack explained. She missed them, she was crying—but she couldn't keep calling his cell, not from bloody China.

"I thought you had unlimited minutes," Jack's older brother said.

"China!" said his wife.

"She's a cocktail waitress," Karla explained, but this seemed unfair. "At the Palace," she added.

"Hostess," Jack corrected.

"How nice of her to call," said Jack's mother.

"Not so nice on his dime," said Jack's father, borrowing a Karla phrase.

"After nine," Jack explained. "That's when the unlimited minutes begin."

Jack got up to root for a beer in the kitchen, and the talking ceased. On TV, Jennifer Saunders was consuming an entire bottle of vodka to a laugh track.

"You should've let me talk," Karla said quietly, when he returned.

"She'll call again." He shrugged and cracked off the bottle cap in his palm.

THE SHOWER DRAIN in the upstairs bathroom was blocked up with Karla's hair. She bought a bottle of Drāno during a morning run and stashed it under the guest bed. She kept a bottle of wine there, too, and a tiny red splotch had stained the pale green carpet where the cork had leaked. She scrubbed the carpet with tonic water, but the splotch was still there.

She offered to help with Sunday dinner and burned the Yorkshire puddings.

"No matter," said Jack's mom, but it did matter—the puddings were everyone's favorite.

She brought home the *Independent* because it came with a Daily Poem and Jack's father asked, smiling, if she was a Communist.

She called Liza and reached her voice mail. She tried to sound chipper, non-desperate in her message. She spelled out Jack's cell phone number clearly, twice.

———

KARLA RECEIVED the first of many long letters from Margaret, written during breaks at the Sky Bar on Palace stationery in looped, determined handwriting. Margaret didn't like e-mail. She liked the old-fashioned way, she said. And, she admitted to Karla, the Japanese boyfriend knew her Hotmail password.

I think maybe to move out, Karla read. The boyfriend was always sleeping. *But probably, I won't!*

She was keeping up with her step classes. She invited the new singer, Fat Arms, but she never came. Jasmine were inseparable. *Always together. Even the shopping.* They spent entire days in the Sky Bar recording new tracks. They'd learned twenty new tunes so far, including three Chinese songs.

We miss you, Margaret added. *And also Willow and Sam say hi.*

The next day Karla wrote back, in tiny print, on the back of a York Minster postcard. "If your boyfriend is sleeping, wake him up! And keep writing. I want to hear everything." She addressed it to the Sky Bar.

THERE WAS a Shanghai scene Karla hadn't recorded, something too long for a scrap. She tried to remember the details as she jogged along the Ouse riverbank path.

She and Jack had been in the park together, People's Square. It had been a gorgeous day, the first warm one in a while, and the new sunshine made everything look better. It was the first time Jack had been there.

Karla had a book and a camera and a pencil and pad, but it was nice just to sit and watch the kites and feel the sun. She was thinking of hummus wraps, spring in college—how she and her roommate had taken their lunch trays outside, ignoring the STAY OFF THE GRASS signs, which someone had decorated with Magic Marker marijuana leaves. She remembered the glare and the persistent bees swarming around trash cans. She remembered sitting on the damp ground cross-legged, in shorts.

She said nothing of this to Jack. He would ask what a hummus wrap was. He would wonder why they couldn't sit on the grass.

Jack was thinking about kites, and he told her so. He explained the difference between normal kites and stunt kites, and where he'd flown them as a kid. He'd been good with kites, better than his brothers.

They watched together as the kite flyers in People's Square swooped and ran—all the colors and the determined faces of children and the drama of tangled string. Karla had no burning desire to be part of it. She thought of the song from *Mary Poppins* and began to hum.

But Jack wanted to have a go. He bought a blue one from a wandering vendor for twelve yuan and said, "Get up. I'm going to teach you."

It took them a while, but eventually it lifted. Everyone had advice. A boy tugged on their string and pointed into the wind. Old ladies shook their heads. And then a girl of nine or ten appeared—boyish haircut, worn, yellow shirt. She had a shy, trusting smile, and she laughed at Karla and Jack in the kindest possible way. When the string snapped, the girl knotted the pieces back together. When it got stuck in a short tree, she pleaded in Mandarin for Jack to retrieve it. He did, and muddied his shoes in the process, and swore accordingly.

And then the girl's father came, in a sweat suit. His own kite was shaped like an owl. He spoke quickly to the girl and gave her a little bag of dried fruit and steered her away. "Okay!" said the girl, waving, and was gone.

Then a man in a suit asked to fly it. He handed over his briefcase—collateral—and ran from them quickly, the kite flapping behind.

Karla and Jack sat on a bench and waited.

"I was thinking of something," said Jack. "Just today, actually, in the loo."

"A helpful detail," said Karla.

"I'm serious. I've got this—plan. I've come up with something. A Life Plan."

A JOE act in every Chinese hotel. A beer that has no calories.

"By thirty-five I want a big house somewhere, not a terraced house but a big one, with lots of friends around."

You're thirty-two. You've got three more years.

"I'm thirty-two, so I haven't got long."

"It doesn't *have* to be by thirty-five," said Karla. She sensed something else was coming. She wanted to delay it.

"It's odd because I've never really wanted that kind of thing before." He held his lighter in his hand and rubbed at the metal switch. "So now that I have this kind of—goal, I suppose, I want to start working toward it."

He paused.

Karla tried to brush away a grass stain on the knee of her jeans.

"I see you in the house."

"I was wondering about that," Karla said. At the same time, she wondered exactly when and where she'd acquired the grass stain.

"You're definitely in the house. If you want to be." He

looked at her. His breath had the familiar burnt sugar smell of booze burning off. His eyes were bright, bright green, his hangover eyes. It was unsettling just how green they were.

"I want to be in the house," Karla said back, and she knew as she spoke that it wasn't the exact truth, just like the duo promise on the crew deck, the last time she'd agreed to follow his plan. (Sonny and Cher, Ike and Tina, Donny and Marie—what had she been thinking? It hadn't worked out for any of them.) It *should've* been the truth. It would've been so much easier if it was.

She touched the hairs on his arm; she plucked at them. Kite flyers and roller skaters circled and adorable kids bobbed with moms and couples walked slowly and the fountain was flowing. Classical music blared from scratchy, invisible speakers.

The businessman didn't return. His briefcase was brown leather, worn, and Jack held it in his lap. "Should we take a look inside?"

"No," Karla said, and together they got up to find him.

The sun was low, and the air was getting chillier. "Mind," said Jack, "it's a good time of day for kites, once we track the bugger down. The wind—" But Karla wanted a beer and a sweater, in that order. She told him so.

They found the man by the fountain, happily coiling string, oblivious to the possibility of theft. He'd weighed the kite tail down with a one-yuan coin.

"Everyone's an expert," Jack said.

"*Sheh sheh,*" said the man, and walked away swinging his case.

Jack wrapped the pieces up carefully—the coin, the kite, the string—and gripped them tightly in his hand to make them stay that way. Then they hailed a cab to O'Farley's for happy hour.

✦

IN YORK KARLA AND JACK went to the Horse and Hare. Their first drinks stood before them, untouched. Willow had called again, during Karla's morning run, and Jack had something to tell her.

"She's pregnant," Jack blurted.

"I know," said Karla. "Margaret told me months ago."

"Months ago?"

"I didn't want you to think less of her."

And then, quite suddenly, she knew, or thought she knew. *Willow's boyfriend.*

"You're a real motherfucker," she said quickly, before she had a chance to change her mind.

Jack blinked. "What?"

"I'm going back home," she added. Enough, already. She would make it impossible for him to divert her.

The Horse and Hare regulars were looking at them. There was a piano in the corner but no pianist. There was a jukebox, large and too bright for the bar, and "Peaceful Easy Feeling" was playing. Jack's face, meanwhile, was working to digest it all.

"You," Karla explained. "Fucking the waitress. Take *her* to your fucking house." Karla's anger surprised her. It seemed unstoppable. It felt summoned from somewhere vast and endless—a Grand Canyon of shittiness. It felt, she had to admit, invigorating to let it seep out.

He was looking at her. With some hatred, yes, but his eyes were on her, focused.

She kept going. "Did you hear me? I lied about the house."

But Jack didn't want to hear this part. His eyes were becoming wilder. "The baby is fucking Marcello's," he said.

"That's not what Margaret told me," said Karla.

"And how would she know?"

"*I* know. Because you flirted with her. Every night. Because—"

"Because you're a paranoid, jealous bitch," he said.

"She keeps calling you," said Karla. She was losing steam, but she had to go on speaking. "You won't let me talk, you won't—"

And then, incredibly, the phone rang. It was Liza. She had a gig for them in Barbados, in a resort near Bridgetown. All found, and they could leave in two weeks. Karla heard it all across the table, the cell phone volume on high, Liza's tinny voice blaring.

"We'll have a think on it," Jack said, and hung up.

"I was going to suggest," he said evenly, "that we pass on the next contract. Stay in York for a while, look for a place. That's what I wanted to talk to you about." Try real life, he meant. He looked at her steadily and then looked away.

The jukebox ran out. No one got up to make it play.

"I had nothing to do with her," Jack said at last, to his hands. "Please, Kar." The offer still stood, he meant. They could laugh about this, try to make up again. It was entirely up to her.

Why? Why was it up to her? It had unraveled so long ago. She saw the damage in its entirety, the whole four sloppy years, done, with or without Willow.

"I think I'm going home," she said. She didn't know what she meant by this, but she understood that it didn't include him. It didn't include Northern Lights. Jack seemed to understand this, too. She could see it in his shoulders, stooped, as though he'd suffered a blow. As though something in him had been released.

Karla would have preferred a cinematic ending, a slamming of doors, a taxi straight to the airport. But there were practical considerations: her things, her plane ticket, a story to devise for their parents, who would probably never know the whole truth.

And so she walked back to the guest bedroom in Jack's house and began to panic in earnest. (Jack stayed at the pub. Before she'd gone he'd ordered a whiskey and ginger and downed it quickly. He drew large, slow circles on the table with his forefinger and said nothing for a long time. Then he touched her wrist and apologized for not sleeping with her anymore. When she got up to leave, he didn't ask her to stay.)

Karla pulled the floral duvet over her head until it was hard to breathe. She imagined waking in her old room in Maine. The dog would paw at her door, and she would think it was the dry cleaning, at first, delivered by Housekeeping. She'd wake with the stuffed animals her mother had preserved—a polar bear with only one eye, a porcupine—and she'd clutch at them, sunlight creeping in through a crack in the curtains. The crack would be wrong—horizontal. Window quilts, installed in 1978 to save on Maine heating bills.

She'd hear her dad's voice on the phone upstairs. (Why was he speaking at that hour? He knew she could hear—she'd always been able to hear.)

"It's hard for the parents when this happens," he'd say to an aunt or an uncle or a cousin. "You get to know a person. And such pretty voices, the two of them. But—"

And this was how he'd leave it, nipping the bad thing in the bud with a hopeful conjunction, letting it dangle.

We did sing pretty together, Karla would think, in her teenage room below, and then she'd finish the dangle. She wouldn't be able to help herself. *But his vowels were fucked up. They were never like mine.*

She couldn't go back to Maine. She'd need something distracting, scary, new. She'd need to be overwhelmed with adjustments and details.

Beyond the guest bedroom, she heard Jack's father flush the toilet and close the bathroom door behind him. The wine under the bed was gone, and Karla longed for a deep, fuzzy slug.

FOURTEEN

Rodgers and Hart

New York, New York, 1999

KARLA FORCED HERSELF to go to the Met and then stayed there all afternoon, until her legs ached. On the way back, she got lost. She thought for sure the 6 train was on Park Avenue. She knew she should ask someone, but she didn't.

Jack would ask, she thought. *He'd be charming and they'd love his accent and they'd tell him exactly how to get there.*

She had a wallet-size map of Manhattan, and she made herself look at it. She stood out of the way and squinted, and the streets she needed were printed right there and soon she was back in her new neighborhood. The Amish Market, which she hadn't been to, where she could buy fresh fruit and vegetables. The 24 Hour Adult Video Store. The Western Union, where she could Get Cash Fast. The Electric Banana Bar, open all day.

She climbed the two flights; she opened her two tricky locks (turn right for top, left for bottom). She filled her kettle and sat in her black folding chair and looked out her better window, one of two in her thousand-dollar-a-month studio apartment. There was an elementary school to the left and a construction site around the corner. There was a new Thai restaurant next door with a tiny beer garden. If Karla opened her window, she would let in fumes and black dust and fragments of happy hour conversation, and so she kept her window closed. She reread the rejection letter on her fridge door, from the Portland School of Art. The letter encouraged her to "distance herself from the snapshot image" and focus on subject matter that was more personally revealing. (*So teach me,* she wanted to reply.) They would welcome a future application, once her perspective was broader.

In the morning Karla would take the subway uptown to her temp job. This month, as a telemarketer for a theater academy, she called random high school students in Georgia and Mississippi and Louisiana—she'd been assigned the southern states—and asked if they were interested in an arts scholarship. It was a trick question because there were no instant scholarships. There were application fees, and it was her job to secure three per day, minimum.

Karla's boss was impressed with her performance background. "You'll be able to relate," he said. "These kids have big plans."

SHE WENT TO Chinatown on Saturday and stopped to look at a smooth jade necklace in an open-front stall. All the souvenirs she brought back from Shanghai—there they were, row upon row.

———

KARLA MADE herself answer an ad in *Back Stage:* "Singers wanted for Broadway Choir."

"I used to sing on cruise ships," she found herself saying on the phone.

"Great!" said the other phone voice. "I'm a Broadway person. Are you a Broadway person?"

"I sang on ships," she tried again. "And in hotels."

"Great!" The Broadway person had no idea what Karla meant by this.

"In lounges. Five-star hotels." Karla summoned all the catchphrases she could muster. "I sang with—a band. I was the lead singer in the band." This sounded better.

"Jazz? Standards? Musical theater?"

"Yes, a mix of material. We had a very large repertoire. Nearly five hundred songs."

"Wow," said the voice, not believing her, but she was invited to audition. She'd have to sight-read and prepare sixteen bars of something upbeat. No ballads.

Karla considered "Moondance," and then decided against it. She'd do the jazziest upbeat song she knew, a standard: "Lady Is a Tramp."

The phone voice belonged to a striking brunette a full head taller than Karla. She looked ageless, probably between twenty-five and forty. She let Karla do the sight-reading part twice. They needed altos, and she was in.

Rehearsals were held in a rented dance studio in Midtown, at 5:00 P.M. sharp. The Broadway people could then dash off, an hour and a half later, to their nearby shows. The non-Broadway people tended to rush off, too, wanting to appear busy. Everyone there had the slightly crazed look that came from trying too hard, from smiling too much. And the voices around her—clear, vibrant, supported by solid diaphragms and years of private training—were much louder than Karla's. She was unmiked now. She had to remind herself to sing the notes as written, without poppy ornamentation. No one there was impressed by Mariah Carey. They sang an experimental version of "The Rime of the Ancient Mariner" in which the altos repeated "I shot the Albatross" for twenty bars straight. The soloist, an ensemble member from *Chicago*, stood on her chair and sang with jazzy, outstretched hands.

Karla stopped going.

She looked at pictures after work, if she'd had enough to drink. There was one that had been her favorite, just her on a Caribbean beach—Tobago, maybe. She wore a washed-out bikini that looked nearly flesh-colored. Fellow sunbathers had looked twice to make sure she wasn't naked.

The day had been overcast, but the right beachy trappings were there—a few lush palm trees, empty white sand, the suggestion of surf nearby (Karla's hair, wet and sea-stringy). She stood with her arms outstretched, her wrists tilted like those of a ballerina, her front leg pointed deliberately. It was the end point for the Top Hat and Tails routine, the stance Karla would take hundreds of times, early show and late show, downstage right.

The picture was meant to be a joke—the photographer, Holly, stood downstage left in the very same position, and this had made them conspirators that day, mocking their lovely profession, miles from the job they had to return to later. Karla glowed in the photo, cocky and tan, still technically unattached to Jack or to anyone.

On the way to her telemarketing job, Karla caught herself in the endless shop windows. Her eyes were too big, and the rest of her was shrinking, not just the twenties baby fat leaving her but her smile, her eyes—everything was tighter, her face framed by a severe ponytail, by a crease-free collar of a benign Gap blouse. She looked nothing at all like a beach Rockette.

MARGARET KEPT writing letters, and through Margaret, Karla was able to imagine endings.

Margaret wrote, *Sam has now a brand-new dog.*

Sam took the dog on walks after work, in a tired daze, glad to be out of the Sky Bar, glad to have a reason to move quickly down the street as morning bled very slowly into the city.

He took longer and longer breaks during his shifts at the Sky Bar, and he scheduled these breaks around happy hours at various hotels: Tuesday, the Portman, Wednesday, the Ritz-Carlton. He wanted to try Yangzi Suites, but it was a little too far. Sam asked the taxi driver to hurry, please, drive faster—he didn't have long. He was almost caught twice, by Rolly, who asked him where he'd been.

"Storeroom," Sam said, and he began to use very strong breath mints.

Sam was promoted eventually, to Wine Buyer. He declined, and cashed in his savings and took his dog on the train to Hangzhou, where he rented a small house a mile from West Lake. He began to carve animals from soapstone (as a boy his father had taught him), and he sold his figurines to tourists. He drank less beer and took longer walks.

He forgot about the American-British duo, who'd been

much like the next duo and the next, reluctant to sing Chinese songs and complaining always about the price of drinks or the lack of customers or the bad weather.

CASH RETURNED to the Sky Bar on business. He had a brief affair with a Singaporean woman who stole his credit card. She refused to call him Pang, although he asked her to, repeatedly. It wasn't her language, and she was tired of being mistaken for a Chinese person.

THE LADY IN GREEN had been drugged the night she was physically removed from the Sky Bar. This is what she told people. A week later she shaved her head, removed her green nail polish, purchased a platinum blond wig, and spent several thousand yuan on leather items: skirt, pants, jacket, bustier. She began to frequent the Yangzi Suites lobby lounge and continued to request "Candle in the Wind." The Yangzi clientele were older by a few decades, and the duo couldn't sing very well. One seemed to be Scandinavian and one was not.

Three months later she quit the hotel circuit and returned to Tongji University to complete her degree in anthropology. She began to date Charles the guitarist and was invited up to the restaurant stage to sing harmonies when he played Beatles songs. In this way she became half of a duo.

FLYNN AND GLO tried to get a gig at the Sky Bar, but Rolly had a strong aversion to Scandinavians (and, Glo suspected, to Flynn), and so they opted to renew their contract at the Yangzi as the Lobby Act. They learned five new songs in three months. They were banned from Heaven Café. Glo thought she was pregnant for a brief time, during which Flynn proposed and vowed to quit drinking. When the pee test came out negative, Glo was relieved, as was Flynn, and they marked the occasion by doing tequila shots in their hotel room.

CHARLES SPENT more and more time at the Forever Pleasure Hall of Paradise Palace. He'd seen *Titanic* twelve times. He took his daughter there, and she ate her popcorn slowly. She liked Kate Winslet's long, pretty hair. She held her father's hand when she was done eating, her small, greasy fingers dwarfed by his big, American hand.

He'd met someone, a singer and anthropologist, two for the price of one! He was in love again, and when Celine Dion's song played through the Palace speakers, he wept quietly, grateful.

ROLLY DIDN'T hate Scandinavians, exactly. In fact, he was an ABBA fan. Northern Lights had done a decent version of "Dancing Queen," and he'd requested it often. He disguised his handwriting and dropped the request cards on the bar, where they were picked up and delivered to the stage by the lovely Willow. The frequent requests gave Jack the opportunity to tell his one ABBA joke: "I always fancied the blond one. (Beat.) And the girls were quite nice as well," which Rolly had found amusing the first few times.

He didn't hire Gin Fizz because the singer's breasts were too large. (Beat.) And she was nothing much to look at, either.

BETH WOULD GO to Boston University as an exchange student for one semester. Karla's parents had written the required sponsorship letter to the admissions office.

"Does it cost anything?" Karla had asked.

"It doesn't appear to," Karla's mother had confirmed.

Beth had sent a thank-you note in return. She e-mailed updates to Karla in the weeks leading up to her departure: her roommate's name, her course schedule, her flight number. And, by the way, could Karla pick her up at Logan Airport?

"I'm sorry," Karla wrote. "But New York is far from Massachusetts. There's probably a bus that will take you straight to your dorm."

"Could I visit you in New York? I would very much like to see the Big Apple City!"

"Let me know how you settle in," Karla responded.

"And your parents, in Maine. I should want to meet them, to thank them in person."

"They're working quite hard at the moment—it's a busy time of year for them."

You're on your own, Karla meant. *And stop being such a user.*

But you promised! Beth thought. *My mother fed you home-made dumplings. And you said I would have fresh Maine lobster, all I could eat.*

MR. MARCELLO, back in Rome, thought of Willow daily. He continued to send checks, and he asked Willow to send letters in return, addressed to his workplace. His e-mail account was not secure. He asked her to meet him in Florence for the weekend, but she couldn't, of course—she didn't have the visa to leave.

The baby, he was fairly certain, was his.

MRS. MARCELLO discovered a stack of letters in her husband's gym bag, letters with Shanghai stamps, addressed in young, pretty handwriting. She read them all, twice, and put them back in the very same order. She said nothing about them to anyone.

Mrs. Marcello considered inventing letters of her own to leave in a drawer for her husband's discovery. She'd cheated on her husband only once, with her tennis coach in the sauna. It had been wonderful but brief, because of the heat.

Instead, she began to make love to Mr. Marcello again. Mr. Marcello thought of Willow and Mrs. Marcello thought of Willow and, alternately, the tennis coach, and occasionally both at the same time, and in this way Mr. and Mrs. Marcello became friendly again, bonded by the other people they conjured, a quartet of bodies half real, half imagined.

WILLOW WAS required to write weekly letters to Mr. Marcello, now that he'd moved back to Italy to live with his wife and children. By this time he'd secured an apartment for her in Pudong, not far from her mother's home, with television sets in every room. He paid for her classes in computers and in English, and she brought her letters to her teacher to proofread. She told the teacher Mr. Marcello was twenty-three and single and a disc jockey at a famous nightclub in Rome.

Meanwhile, Willow grew bigger. Her feet swelled and would no longer fit into her nice, suede shoes.

She received long, confusing e-mail messages from Karla, who wrote about a choir and a job where she talked on the phone all day in New York City. Willow thought about asking her English teacher to translate in more detail but decided against it. The messages made her feel stupid and very far away.

"Forget the Americans, the Italians—they're always leaving," said Willow's mother, who came to Willow's apartment nightly. She cooked for her daughter and filled a large plastic bowl with hot water. She told Willow to soak her swollen feet and to practice her breathing exercises. She chopped scallions and waited for the baby to arrive.

Her daughter was at the computer, looking at a blue screen called "Hotmail."

"I've already forgotten," said Willow, who, in her own language, knew she would be just fine. She was hungry, and she wished her mother would hurry up with the dinner. She wished the baby would hurry up and come. She touched her new, hard belly, and then she deleted Karla's messages, one by one.

KARLA TOOK THE Port Authority bus to Elizabeth, New Jersey, to the nearest IKEA. The bus was free, and this was exciting to Karla, who was beginning to learn just how rare New York freebies were. It was Sunday, and the bus was filled with young, sleepy couples and single women with large paper cups of coffee. One sat beside Karla, not with coffee but with chai tea.

"It smells much better than it tastes," the woman admitted. She said her name was Vanessa. She had neatly clipped bangs and chunky, silver earrings. She looked older than Karla by about three years.

"What are you getting?" Karla asked.

"Plant holders and an ironing board," said Vanessa. "And a frying pan if they're cheap."

"I saw one in Bed Bath and Beyond," Karla said. "A frying pan. I don't need one."

"What do you need?"

Karla had a list prepared, a list left over from lazy Palace

Hotel mornings. What did she need? In Shanghai she'd wanted a bookshelf, a dishwasher, a dishcloth, tiny kisses on her spine, a firm hand grabbing her ass out of nowhere, a breathy *"Baby,"* a set of Tupperware containers (one snugly locked inside the other), a good bagel with cream cheese, a bright IKEA catalog on an IKEA coffee table. It was how she woke up sometimes in Shanghai, thinking of IKEA.

"I need a CD rack," she told Vanessa. "Maybe a cutting board."

She'd found the IKEA catalog her mother had sent, with the earmarked page, Karla's favorite room. It had been shoved in an old lyrics folder, the lyrics long since memorized. The room was done in whites and blues, white curtains billowing out like sails, as if the ocean had swept itself in and stayed there. There were bleached glassy things in decorative jars and bare, shiny, wooden floors, and all the chairs were placed at pleasing angles. There were books neatly lined in shelves that rose to the ceiling and a desk in the corner, her own desk, and a lamp like a robot arm that moved out of the way easily with a small, careless nudge.

She could have these things. She could construct the perfect room. She had a credit card, she was on the bus, she was going to New Jersey.

"Pot holders," Karla added. "Throw pillows."

"Nice," said Vanessa.

Karla sipped her coffee without scalding her tongue. She could smell Vanessa's tea—nutmeg and marshmallows. "What do you think of beach glass?" Karla asked. She was prepared to explain what she meant by this. Not everyone knew.

"I like it," said Vanessa. "My mother does that, in little jars on window ledges."

"Exactly," said Karla, and they rode in silence the rest of the way.

THE LETTERS FROM Margaret came less often. When they did come, Karla made tea and sat by the window to read slowly. She ripped open the thick Palace envelopes carefully with her thumb.

The baby has come now, Margaret reported, *and Willow is skinny again, already. Baby is fine and lucky to be born this year, year of the Rabbit. Her name is Daisy.*

What is her Chinese name? Karla wanted to know.

Too tricky to tell you, Margaret would reply. *But you can call her Daisy.*

✧

THERE WAS ONE ending left. Karla took her time with it.

JACK GOT HIS HOUSE, not in York but in Dubai, where he'd been hired, despite Liza's protests, as Entertainment Manager for a brand-new hotel on Sheikh Zayed Road. He did his research and flirted with real estate agents and saw dozens of pink-marbled condos before he found it, an actual house: four bedrooms, two solid stories, enough space for his siblings and parents to stay all at once. There was a tremendous yard, a swimming pool, a wraparound porch, creamy hardwood floors, and a little bar in the living room. Stools with red leather cushions. Daily sun streaming in.

Karla had never been able to adjust to the brightness there, the sun hurling itself down on objects, the way night offered no real coolness, the buildings and roads having sucked up sun all day. But Jack liked it, the constant warmth.

In the evening, when the prayers began and the wailing echoed across his fertilized yard, he liked to take his pint glass outside and sit by the pool. He stayed there for hours, letting the heat make him tired, watching the light disappear from the vast, Persian sky.

✧

KARLA STARTED thinking about Maine, once her apartment was perfectly decorated. She thought of *Carousel,* the movie. She couldn't help it. She remembered the blue-gold spangle of sea and sun and the handstands and hornpiping of "June Is Bustin' Out All Over." On her day off she took the C train to the South Street Seaport, where the cobblestone streets and cheery, empty shops reminded her of Portland's Old Port. At the wharf, the big, dead schooner *The Peking* was locked into the pier and open for tours.

She watched a water taxi shoot across the river to New Jersey.

Someone joined her on the bench, a gray-haired woman in a sarong, and then someone sat next to the woman, a guy in a Red Sox baseball cap, though the bench was made for only two. The whole pier was filling up—kids with ice-cream cones and parents with cups of beer and buskers with guitars and a mime dressed like the Statue of Liberty, her arm raised, her skin painted copper green.

Then Karla saw why they'd come. It was a beast of a thing—white, gleaming, ten decks high at least, no company name that she could see, probably on the Jersey side. Having left its West Side berth, the ship inched easily down the Hudson.

ACKNOWLEDGMENTS

I'M GRATEFUL TO the many Hoteliers and Entertainers who inspired me along the way, including the warm and astute Cruise Director who told me "a smile costs nothing." Thanks to the curators of the Shanghai Museum, circa 1998, who inscribed "Pottery belongs to all mankind, but porcelain is China's invention" on the wall of the Ceramics wing.

At Anne Edelstein Literary Agency, thanks to the tenacious Emilie Stewart for sticking with Karla and Jack. Thanks to Anne Edelstein for inviting me in.

At Harcourt, thanks to Stacia Decker for her insightful edits and her appreciation for duos. Thanks to Sarah Melnyk for seeing me as more than a chick.

Thanks to my smart and generous writing teachers in Swannanoa—Judith Grossman, C. J. Hribal, Jim Shepard, and Joan Silber (the four J's)—for insisting that cruise ships are cool. Thanks to Bill Roorbach, for knowing that Maine is cool, too.

Thanks to Random House for use of A. S. Byatt's wise words.

I would like to thank The Eagles and Paul Simon for their use of material, but I can't. (They didn't grant permission.)

Thanks to Tupper and Tupper and the Essex Street Esquire for legal counsel.

Thanks to Robert Mitchell for making sharp pictures at cold Ocean Point.

Thanks to my earliest editor, Chelsea Farley, and to Mireille Abelin, Carol Ghiglieri, Krista Jack, Laura Pinsof, and Laurie Wainberg, for brunch support, chips and salsa support, and/or long-distance enthusiasm.

Thanks to Audrey and Miles Reben for endless rounds of Stink Pink.

Thanks to David Parker Purcell, who keeps me listening to all the good music.

Thanks to Mom, for being an insatiable reader.

Thank you, Dad, for the ukulele, for Willie Nelson, for loving me so.